Penelope

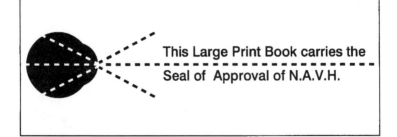

Penelope

Marion Chesney

Thorndike Press • Waterville, Maine

Published in 2002 by arrangement with Lowenstein Associates, Inc.

Thorndike Press Large Print Romance Series.

The tree indicium is a trademark of Thorndike Press.

The text of this Large Print edition is unabridged.
Other aspects of the book may vary from the original edition.

Set in 16 pt. Plantin.

Printed in the United States on permanent paper.

Library of Congress Cataloging-in-Publication Data

Chesney, Marion.
    Penelope / Marion Chesney.
        p. cm.
    ISBN 0-7838-9604-2 (lg. print : hc : alk. paper)
    1. Large type books.   I. Title.
PR6053.H4535 P44 2002
    823'.914—dc21   2001051442

For Harry Scott Gibbons
and Charles David Bravos Gibbons
With Love

Chapter One

Miss Augusta Harvey let out a long sigh of satisfaction which ended in a discreet belch. In front of her the waxed floor of the ballroom mirrored the feathers and silks and jewelry of the *haut ton*.

"I have arrived," she said to her shivering companion, Miss Euphemia Stride. "I have indeed arrived. You have done well, Euphemia."

And Miss Stride, a faded spinster in her fifties, felt she had indeed done well. It was not everyone who could secure an invitation to the Courtlands' ball for the vulgar and pushing Augusta Harvey who had managed to alienate practically all of London society since her arrival in town a mere few weeks before.

Euphemia would hardly have dared risk society's displeasure by thrusting such a mushroom as Miss Harvey on them had it not been for the generous bribe offered her by that lady. Even then she had not found the courage to inform the Courtlands of the name of the "friend" she was bringing to their ball. Perhaps it would not be so bad. Augusta looked quite the thing in a heavy crêpe evening gown with a vandyked hem and a fine row of pearls embellishing her fat neck. If only she would keep her mouth shut!

It was then, as Euphemia surveyed Miss Harvey's gown, that she noticed the first disaster of the evening.

"My dear Augusta," she whispered desperately, "you have *straw* clinging to your hem. Do but remove it before anyone sees."

"Pooh! What does it matter?" said Miss Harvey, plucking off the offending straw. But with a sinking heart Miss Stride noticed several of the chaperones had already noticed the straw and were whispering together, turbans and feathers nodding. The damage was done. Straw on one's skirt meant that one had arrived in a hack, which was exactly what the cheese-paring Augusta had done, instead of renting a carriage as Euphemia had earnestly advised.

In fact, reflected Miss Euphemia Stride bitterly, Augusta could well afford to keep her own carriage. Goodness knows, the way Augusta had gained her wealth was disgraceful and scandalous enough without attracting the added censure of society.

Augusta Harvey had been nurse and housekeeper to a wealthy mill owner whom she had bullied into an apoplexy. He had conveniently died from it, leaving her sole heir to his great fortune. His relatives had unsuccessfully tried to contest the will and had claimed that Augusta had poisoned the old man. But the triumphant Augusta had left them to their fury and had travelled to London to realise her lifelong ambition — to become a society lady.

But society had been strangely reluctant to allow her past their doors; Miss Stride had been the only one who would even take a bribe. And luckily for Augusta, the woman was a distant relative of the Courtlands, whose ball, two weeks before the official opening of the London Season, was held to be a great event.

Augusta's gooseberry green eyes surveyed the ballroom. She had arrived late in order to make an entrance and had just realised that by so doing she had missed being received by her hostess. She accordingly urged the shrinking Euphemia to present her to Lady Courtland.

Miss Stride looked to right and left like a trapped animal, but since she desperately needed the money Augusta was to pay her, she stiffened her threadbare velvet spine and led Augusta towards where Lady Courtland was standing.

An extremely tall woman, the Lady looked down at Augusta's crocodile smile with eyes that were as hard and sparkling as her diamonds. Miss Stride gave an apologetic cough and made the introductions. Lady Courtland haughtily held out one finger for Miss Harvey to shake. Augusta, however, seized Lady Courtland by the whole hand and wrung it fervently.

"So pleased," she simpered awfully. " 'Tis so kind of your la'ship to invite me on this montrous genteel occasion."

"I did not invite you," snapped Lady Courtland. "I was under the impression that Miss Stride was bringing a *friend*."

"And so she did, Lor' bless her," said Augusta, putting a fat arm round the cringing Euphemia Stride. "Me and Euphie is the *dearest* of friends."

Now Miss Harvey was a prey to flatulence, and her embarrassing malady suddenly decided to overtake her. A sound worthy of Wellington's artillery at Salamanca rattled from beneath her skirts and slowly raising a perfumed handkerchief to her nose, Lady Courtland turned and walked majestically away. Euphemia dragged

Augusta to the side of the ballroom.

Miss Stride resolved to make the best of things. She would suffer the evening, take Augusta's money, and never, *never* set eyes on that repellent woman again. But first she had to earn her money. She set herself to please by pointing out various notables. There was my Lord Alvanley and there was the Countess Lieven and that very handsome man was the Earl of Hestleton. And there was little Miss Parsey . . .

"Parseys are in trade. Merchants," said Miss Harvey. "How did she get here?"

"Because," explained Miss Stride, "Miss Parsey is engaged to young Lord Wellcombe and *that* makes a difference. One can often get entrée to the best families through marriage. Now if you were younger . . ." Miss Stride's voice trailed off, and she allowed herself the luxury of a malicious titter.

"Well, I ain't," said Augusta slowly, "but Penelope is."

"Who's Penelope?"

"Niece of mine," remarked Miss Augusta, staring at the dancing figures. "She's working at some seminary in Bath as a governess. Beautiful girl. An orphan. Do you think she . . . ?"

"Oh, of course! What a good idea!" exclaimed Euphemia Stride, who privately

11

thought that Miss Harvey would need a great deal more than a beautiful niece to make even the smallest crack in the social world.

"I'll see," said Augusta. "I'll see. Meanwhile I may as well move about and meet these grand folks."

"I wouldn't do that," exclaimed Miss Stride in dismay.

"Why not?" said Miss Harvey. "You saw how civil Lady Courtland was with me." And to Miss Stride's horror she wandered off in the direction of the row of chaperones.

"How do," said Augusta cheerfully, smiling her widest until her teeth seemed to stretch to her ears. "May I present myself? I am a great friend of Lady Courtland."

The lady she had addressed sat looking up into Augusta's glittering smile as if she could not believe her eyes. Now the Baroness Delsey was not a particularly aggressive or malicious woman, but the sight of the beaming Augusta was too much for her.

"Go away. Shooo!" said the Baroness, flapping her fan. "I declare, the Courtlands' cook has come a-visiting!" The hard eyes of the row of chaperones bored into Augusta's protruding green ones and even the thick-skinned Augusta felt obliged to retreat.

12

She swept through the double doors of the ballroom and stood irresolute in the hall. When Penelope was married to a Duke, why, then, they would sing a different tune. She realised with a start that in her mind she had already invited Penelope to London.

And to make up for some of the cost of bringing her niece to town, she would cut Euphemia's fee by half, that she would! The woman should have organised things better.

Still smarting from humiliation, Augusta decided to indulge in her favorite hobby — that of poking her nose into every room and drawer in someone else's house. The upper floors of the house were silent and deserted, every available servant having been pressed into service downstairs. Though the house was mainly early Georgian in design, it had had a good few bits and pieces of annexes tacked on since it was first built. It was much larger than even the imposing front-age on Grosvenor Square had led Miss Harvey to expect.

She pottered through bedroom and study, her nimble, podgy fingers slipping various little objects into her reticule, a snuffbox here, a fan there. She ambled along the silent corridors, occasionally cocking her great befeathered head for the footsteps of an approaching servant. Ambling into a private sitting room, she immediately noticed a pretty little enamelled snuffbox on an occasional table in front of a blazing fire and a silver tray with several decanters. She helped herself to the snuffbox and then to a goblet of brandy.

Despite the crackling fire and the decanters, the sitting room carried the musty, airless smell of disuse. Had probably not been used since the Courtlands' ball last year, thought Augusta, and was now only put in readiness for some houseguest. She had just withdrawn the snuffbox from her now bulging reticule to assess its value when she heard the sound of voices in the corridor outside. Clutching the snuffbox, she looked round wildly and then espied a Chinese lacquered screen in the shadowy corner over by the fire. When the door swung open, she was safely behind it, trying to control her heavy breathing.

Two men entered the room. A cultured English voice spoke first.

"I'm glad of the money, demmit, but mark you, it don't seem like treason to me, what with Boney safely locked up in Elba."

"He will return, dear Charles," replied a sibilant, mocking voice with a slight French accent. "In the meantime it is necessary to know the strength of the British forces. You

14

have the list of the regiments in America and the West Indies, I believe."

"Got them here," said the English voice sulkily. "Now hand over the money. I don't know what my brother would say an' he should ever hear of this."

"Your so dear brother, the Earl of Hestleton, would shoot you, dear Charles. Make sure you play our game and keep your mouth shut," intoned the Frenchman with a certain amused indifference.

There was a rustling of paper and the clink of gold. Miss Harvey felt she would die from excitement. A spy! And brother to the Earl of Hestleton at that! Charles. Charles who? Miss Harvey's mind rattled through the pages of the peerage. Viscount Charles Clairmont, that was it! Famous. Behind that screen lay the key to society. But wait a bit. The Hestleton family was famous for their wealth. Why should the Viscount need money?

As if in answer to her unspoken question, the Frenchman went on, "It was indeed lucky for me that you are such an inveterate gambler, dear Charles. Even Charles Fox at his worst could not lose so much money of an evening as you. And promising that stern brother of yours that you would never gamble again was quite silly; it sent you straight into our hands."

"Damn you, you whoreson," grated the Viscount. "If I thought there was any possibility of Napoleon ever escaping from Elba, I would shoot myself. Take your damned, curst, jeering face away. You've got what you want."

"Until the next time," mocked the Frenchman's voice. *"Au revoir."*

The sitting room door slammed.

Miss Harvey edged her large bulk round the screen.

Viscount Clairmont was sitting in front of the fire with his head buried in his hands.

She gave a genteel cough, and the young Viscount straightened up and stared at her in horror.

"Naughty boy!" crowed the apparition in front of him, roguishly wagging a fat finger.

He saw before him a fat woman dressed in green crêpe. She had protruding eyes and a wide mouth which seemed to stretch from ear to ear.

"Let me introduce myself," she beamed. "I am Augusta Harvey and you, I take it, are Viscount Clairmont — a Bonapartiste spy."

"Thank God it's all over," said Viscount Clairmont, getting wearily to his feet and pouring himself a glass of wine. "You may tell my brother what you will, madame."

Miss Harvey kept on smiling. The youth in front of her was, she judged, about nineteen years old, although lines of dissipation had already left their mark on his thin, white face. And, as her crafty eyes noticed the weak mouth and thin, trembling feminine hands, her smile stretched wider and wider.

"But your brother need never know," she said softly.

He gave her a wild look of hope and then his face fell. He said in a flat voice, "I can't pay you. You no doubt heard I am betraying my country to pay my gambling debts, madame."

"Oh, I don't want money," purred Miss Harvey. "No, I've enough of that. But I need an entrée to your household — and your brother."

"Why, in God's name?"

"Because," said Miss Harvey, coming close to him, "I need all your help. I am going to invite my little niece, Penelope, to London. I am going to bring her out. And *you* are going to do everything you can to help her marry your brother."

The Viscount nearly dropped his glass. "Marry Roger? You must be mad! Roger will never marry. He's five and thirty and has had every debutante and matchmaking mama chasing him since he was out of short coats."

Miss Harvey looked baffled and then mutinous. "Your brother's attitude toward marriage is quite well known. Yet you must do everything in your power to throw your brother and my Penelope together. Or I shall tell him of your spying activities."

For one brave second Charles was on the threshold of telling this ghastly old frump to go to the devil. But surely a little matchmaking was not much to ask?

"Very well, then," he sighed. He looked full at the triumphant Miss Harvey and gave a shudder. "But Roger will think I'm mad."

Sometime later that evening Roger, 6th Earl of Hestleton, looked across the ballroom and found a strange fat lady in green simpering and winking at him.

"Who on earth is that?" he asked his friend, Guy Manton.

Mr. Manton put up his quizzing glass and then lowered it hurriedly. "Looks just like a crocodile, don't she. That's the famous Miss Harvey. Most vulgar, pushing woman anyone has ever met. For God's sake, don't look at her or she'll be round, shoving her

18

way into your house in the morning."

"Relax, my friend," laughed the Earl. "That monstrosity will never set foot in any home of mine!"

Chapter Two

Penelope Vesey was not, in fact, a fully fledged governess. Having been orphaned at the age of sixteen, she was left by her penniless father to the tender mercies of the Misses Fry's Seminary for Young Ladies in Bath, who took in the orphan as an articled pupil. Her pay was some few guineas a year, her duty to teach music to the pupils, and her lot little better than a servant's.

Her father had been Sir James Vesey's youngest son and had disgraced himself at an early age by marrying Penelope's mother, a woman whose connections were considered to be vulgar in the extreme. The sight of Augusta Harvey grinning and simpering at the wedding had been enough for Sir James to vow never to set a foot across his son's threshold, damning all his in-laws as common. He had allowed him a meager yearly allowance and, on the death of his son, the allowance had ceased, Sir James seeming to care nothing for the orphaned Penelope.

Penelope's mother had died of cancer when Penelope was still in her cradle. Her father, a weak and feckless man, had left Penelope to be brought up by a series of slatternly servants. A few days before his death, he had assumed some sort of responsibility towards his daughter by petitioning the Misses Fry to take care of his child should anything happen to him. He died of consumption, coughing up his last breath while his terrified little daughter clutched his hand.

The only relative to attend the funeral was Augusta Harvey who seemed massively indifferent to the plight of the girl. But the Misses Fry had fulfilled their promise — only after discovering that the young Penelope Vesey was an expert musician.

She was popular with the pupils and did not eat much; therefore she was allowed to stay. Her beauty — although unfashionably fair — was at first considered a disadvantage, but since Miss Vesey was not likely to meet any men, with the exception of the elderly dancing master, the Misses Fry coped with that problem by making Penelope wear a series of unbecoming caps and, goodness knows, her dresses were dowdy enough. Her only refuge from the stultifying round of walks and lessons and bad food was in playing the pianoforte in the cold and drafty music room.

It was there that Penelope was sitting one spring day, idly running her fingers over the keys and feeling very sorry for herself indeed. The day was her eighteenth birthday, and she was human enough to resent the fact that it should be a day like any other. "We do not encourage the poorer members of our staff to celebrate their birthdays," the Misses Harriet and Frederica Fry had told her, "lest our more affluent pupils think that they may be soliciting gifts."

I didn't want a gift, thought Penelope, striking a jarring chord. "I only wanted someone to say, Happy Birthday."

She quickly got to her feet, walked over to the window and opened it with a jerk. A light, sweet wind danced into the room, bringing with it all the smells of May; lilac, hyacinth, and hawthorn. The old crab apple tree at the bottom of the garden moved its great branches in the soft wind, sending down a flurry of pink and white blossom across the scrubby lawn. Overcome by a great yearning for she knew not what, she impatiently removed her cap and let the breeze play through her hair.

Penelope began to dream that this tall,

narrow, Queen Anne house with its tall, narrow, dark rooms was her own. The music room behind her changed in her mind's eye as she busily decorated it and furnished it. The bare sanded floor would be waxed to a high shine and covered with oriental rugs. The furniture would be light and spindly, and a great fire would crackle on the hearth to banish the permanent chill of the house. Delicate china bowls, so translucent that you could see your fingers through them, would be filled with spring flowers. There would be fine paintings like Canalettos on the walls, blazing with richness and color. And the door would open. And *he* would be standing there . . . that vague suitor of her dreams.

She gave a guilty start as she heard the door behind her open, and she turned slowly round.

The eldest of the Fry sisters, Miss Harriet, stood framed in the doorway. A small, dumpy woman who affected a hideous style in turbans, she always addressed her remarks to some piece of furniture rather than the person she was supposed to be talking to.

"Miss Vesey," she told the piano severely, "put on your cap and come to my study immediately. My sister and I have some tremendous news for you."

Miss Fry waited nervously until Penelope had extinguished her bright gold curls under her cap. Really the girl's looks were too flamboyant for a teacher.

Penelope meekly followed her to the dark, airless study at the back of the house where Miss Harriet and Miss Frederica Fry held court. Miss Frederica was younger than her sister by two years but was often taken for her twin. She was equally dumpy and furtive and had the same irritating mannerisms as her sister.

"Come in, Penelope," she told the fire irons. "You shall take a dish of Bohea with us to strengthen your nerves for the Great Shock."

Penelope looked at her in a bewildered way and then reflected that having lost a mother and father at least had its grim compensations. There was no one left in the world that she cared for now, so the "Great Shock" could not be the death of a dear one.

Penelope sat primly on the edge of a high-backed chair and accepted a cup of tea. The sisters sat on either side of her. At last Miss Frederica began.

"My dear Penelope. We have *incredible* news for you. Yes. Incredible," she assured the teapot. "Is it not so, Harriet?"

"Yes, indeed," said Harriet earnestly to a bust of Plato. "I declare, I was set all of a *tremble.*"

"Do, *do* have a cake," Miss Frederica urged the chimneypiece.

Penelope stared at the sisters in amazement but hurriedly took a cake. She could not remember when she had last had such a treat since she was not allowed to eat with the pupils or the teachers, and had to take as much, or as little, as the servants allowed her.

With the air of a magician producing a rabbit out of a hat, Miss Frederica suddenly held up a letter. Penelope glanced at it and then ate her cake with simpleminded concentration, wondering if she could possibly just reach forward her hand and take another.

"This," Miss Frederica was assuring the sugar bowl, "is a letter from your aunt, Miss Harvey."

Penelope suddenly felt she would need all the small comfort she could get and courageously took another cake. She had seen Augusta but once, at her father's funeral, and still remembered that lady with a mixture of awe and dislike.

"Miss Harvey," went on the younger Miss Fry, "has invited you to her mansion in

London where you are to make your *come out.*"

Penelope stared wide-eyed in amazement. "Why?" she asked faintly.

"You silly goose," said Miss Frederica good-naturedly, rustling the letter. "Because she is exceeding fond of you. She is a delightful lady. Seventy-five thousand, I've heard. Delightful!"

"But aunt has no money!" exclaimed Penelope.

"She says here," said Miss Frederica, waving the letter, "that she has inherited her late employer's fortune."

Penelope's heart began to beat against her ribs. She did not want to go and live with Augusta. On the other hand a Season could mean a husband, someone young and kind and merry. And then . . . oh bliss! A home of her own. A home with the translucent bowls of flowers and crackling fires and *food,* masses and masses of food. *Hot* food.

The Misses Fry seemed to have taken her assent for granted and talked of school matters while they drank their tea. Penelope did not despise them for their sudden kindness to her now that she was to move up in society. It was only to be expected that they should fawn on her today despite the fact that they were bullying and humiliating her yesterday. It was the way of the world after all. She cheerfully ate two more cakes in quick succession and slipped two more in her pocket for little Mary, the scullery maid who shared Penelope's meager diet. She then cheerfully thanked the sisters for the unexpected treat and retired to her room.

With the eternal optimism of youth, she began to tremble with excitement at the thought of her good fortune. Augusta Harvey was a poisonous, vulgar woman, but she, Penelope, was to have a Season, and she would not be *dancing* with Miss Harvey after all. The older woman would merely be the chaperone in the background.

The news of her good fortune soon spread quickly through the school. The governesses and richer girls who had always treated her with alarming condescension but liked her because she "knew her place" now became very affectionate indeed. Only Mary, the little scullery maid, crying dismally over her present of two cakes in the basement, seemed genuinely sorry that Penelope was leaving.

"I shall send for you, Mary," said Penelope, giving her a fierce hug. "You shall be my lady's maid as soon as ever I am married."

And little Mary's tears had dried because

Miss Penelope was so pretty — why, she would be married after her first ball!

Penelope was lucky in her journey. The road was fair and conditions were good. She was too unused to comfort to mind the jolting of the cumbersome coach and too unaccustomed to compliments to object to the heavy badinage from the men on the roof of the coach, unaware that her air of shy good breeding had spared her from coarser gallantries.

The light was fading as the hack which she had hired outside the Bell Savage rolled into Brook Street. She tipped the jarvey with the last of her meager store of money and shyly walked up the marble steps and knocked timidly on the door.

A powdered footman answered the summons and ushered her into a large drawing room at the front of the house. He then departed to inform Miss Harvey of her arrival.

Penelope timidly looked about her. A thick carpet covered with pink cabbage roses quarrelled noisily with the screaming red and yellow stripes of the furniture. An overornate clock ticked away the seconds like a series of sharp reprimands. A row of Miss Harvey's "ancestors," bought at a country-house sale, stared down into the room as if amazed to find themselves in such vulgar surroundings. Some bad pottery figurines simpered and danced on various little cane tables and bowed to their counterparts on the mantelpiece.

Penelope crossed to the looking glass over the fireplace and frowned at her reflection, carefully removed her shabby bonnet and, finding a comb in her reticule, ran it through her curls.

Miss Harvey was announced, and Penelope swung round. Both women surveyed each other in silence.

Augusta reflected that the girl was much thinner than she had remembered and her face was too pale. But her hair was still as gold and her wide questioning eyes still as deep and startling a blue as they had been when last she saw her niece.

For her part, Penelope was thinking gloomily that Aunt Augusta was much the same despite a new, shiny nut-brown wig, rouged cheeks, and a fine collar of pearls.

"Welcome, my dear," said Augusta, waddling forward. "I can see we'll need to buy you some fine new dresses, heh! Of course it will cost me a prodigious amount of money, but there then, I always was a generous soul. Lady Courtland was only saying to me the other day, 'La! Augusta, if you ain't the soul of generosity,' that she did!

"And of course you ain't the type of gel to forget a bit of Christian gratitude when you is wed to a fine Lord. You'll always remember your old auntie what took you out of the gutter? Course you will," she rattled on before Penelope could protest that the seminary in Bath was hardly the gutter. " 'Cause I'm going to dress you proper. I would've taken care of you before, but I hadn't the money and that's a fact. You'll hear some say I poisoned the old man so's to get his money, but I assure you that was not the case since the old quiz a-took of an apoplexy and died proper in his bed but this is London and them society tongues is wicked."

She actually paused for breath, and Penelope said tremulously, "I am sure I shall always be grateful to you, Aunt."

"That's my girl," wheezed Miss Harvey, plunking her great bulk down on the sofa and smiling from ear to ear. "Now for the best bit of news. Me and you has been asked to none other than the Earl of Hestleton's for dinner tomorrow night. I got a fine dress made up for you but, now that I see you, it'll maybe need taking in a peg or two. Now this here Earl is the catch of the Season and a pretty little thing like you will catch his eye, that's for sure. You're not to pay any attention to his young brother, the Viscount, who is by way of being a friend of mine. 'You're like a mother to me, Augusta,' says the dear boy. So he has told the Earl he wants to entertain us to dinner, but the Earl, he's not too keen on the idea, but as soon as he sets eyes on your loveliness, it'll be right and tight and you leave your auntie to fix the marriage settlements good and proper."

"But, Aunt," protested Penelope. "I do not know this Earl. He may take me in dislike!"

"Then it's up to a clever puss like you to see he does not," said Augusta with her smile at its widest. "I don't want you to be *fast,* mind, but a gel can always do discreet things, you know, bend forward and let your dress slip a little. Discreet little pressure of the hand, heh! Tie your garter and then pretend you didn't know he was in the room, heh!"

Penelope blushed painfully. "I must know, Aunt," she said firmly, "whether you have brought me to London for the soul purpose of seducing this Earl?"

"Lord love you, no! As God is my witness," cried Augusta, raising her dirty, plump arms to the painted ceiling, "it's just

31

such a chance for you!"

Penelope sighed. She found her aunt more pushing and vulgar than she had remembered, but perhaps the Bath seminary had made her too missish in her ideas.

"I will do my best for you, Aunt," Penelope said dutifully.

"That's all I ask," said Augusta. "Just do what Auntie tells you and never forget where your bread and butter comes from or the good Lord above will strike you dead for your ingratitude. He often does that, you know," she added in a conversational voice. "He seeks out the sinner even here in St. James's and He strikes 'em dead as doornails. And you don't want to be a-burning in hellfire with demons a-sticking pitchforks in your naked body, do you? No, I thought not. People don't. So you run off to bed like a good girl — the housekeeper will show you to your room — and get a good night's sleep for we've a great deal of shopping to do on the morrow. Good night, my child, and may the angels attend your rest."

Penelope dutifully kissed the rouged cheek presented to her and meekly followed the housekeeper out and up the wide carpeted stairs to the uncarpeted and sparsely furnished bedroom above. Augusta did not believe in spending money on furnishing the rooms that nobody but the inmates of the house were likely to see.

A few streets away in an elegant mansion in Berkeley Square, Roger, Earl of Hestleton was wrestling with both his cravat and his temper while his young brother lounged in a chair beside the dressing table and watched his efforts.

"Not like you to make such a mull of it," said Charles laconically.

The Earl swore and ripped the muslin from his neck and held out his hand to his valet for another cravat. "If I were not so upset and puzzled by your strange behavior," snapped Roger, "I should have this pesky cravat completed in a trice. As it is, I am taken up with wonder over my dear brother's dinner invitation. I keep asking and asking and each time you become more evasive. Why, pray, is one of London's most pushing mushrooms to grace my dinner table?"

"Oh, she's not so bad and I hear her niece is a beauty," said Charles, shifting in his chair and avoiding his brother's eye in the mirror. "You're not usually so high in the instep."

"Not when it comes to rank," said the Earl, completing the arrangement of his cravat in the Mathematical, "but I certainly am when it comes to manners and elegance of mind and from what I have heard, Augusta Harvey has neither."

"Well . . . well," said Charles, rising to his feet, "the invitation is issued and that's that. It's only one evening, that's all."

"One evening too much," said the Earl, placing a diamond pin carefully in the snowy folds of his cravat and turning abruptly to face his brother. "Are you in dun territory again, Charles? Is this why you are encouraging this woman?"

"No!" said Charles sulkily. "Didn't I give you my word? You could at least trust your own brother's word."

The Earl surveyed him in silence and then a singularly charming smile lit up his harsh features. "Come, now, Charles," he said. "I am not such an ogre that you cannot confide in me. If it is not money, then are you interested in Augusta's niece?"

"No!" shrieked Charles. He then added in a quieter voice, "No. It is just that Augusta Harvey has been exceedingly kind to me. She's not that bad you know, and people are too hard on her. Well, you will see for yourself tomorrow."

He looked hopefully into his brother's rather austere features, and sighed. Charles knew that the Earl would be horrified by Augusta. Charles had not yet met Penelope, but he was sure she would prove to be as impossible as her aunt.

Chapter Three

Penelope was exhausted, bewildered, and hungry by the time the hack deposited her along with her aunt on the Earl of Hestleton's doorstep.

The day had been filled with visits to buy hats, shawls, fans, shoes, dresses, pelisses, and wraps. She had been pushed, prodded, turned, and pinned until her head whirled. Augusta Harvey had not stopped once for meals. "During the Season," she had said with her usual crocodile smile, "you may eat your fill in someone else's house. 'Tis the done thing."

In all this whirl of shopping, Penelope had been torn between gratitude towards her aunt for her splendid new wardrobe and distaste for her vulgar, pushing ways. Madame Verné, the dressmaker, had discreetly suggested that Miss Harvey's niece was in need of new underthings. "Why?" Augusta had demanded with great aplomb. "I ain't wasting money on what don't show."

Now, despite the courage engendered by a beautiful white silk dress embroidered at neck and hem with tiny rosebuds and a completely new coiffeur of artlessly rioting curls, created for her by Monsieur André, the court hairdresser, Penelope heartily wished the evening were over.

She wished this more than ever as they were ushered into the Earl's drawing room. The exquisite furniture, the fine paintings, the beautifully subdued colors — all made Augusta Harvey appear at her worst. Miss Harvey was dressed in all the glory of green and white stripes with a multitude of bows and tucks and flounces.

An applewood fire crackled on the hearth, and two fine chandeliers cast a flattering glow over the room.

Charles lounged into the room, looking self-conscious. His face lightened when he saw Penelope, and he made her his best bow. Penelope saw a pleasant looking young man with a weak face, impeccably dressed in long tails and evening breeches and a cravat so high that he had difficulty turning his head. He sported a great number of fobs and seals on his waistcoat and nervously took snuff in rapid delicate little pinches from an enamelled snuffbox. To Penelope's surprise, the Viscount seemed to be as nervous as she was herself, and she set herself to put him at his ease, asking him questions on London life and succeeding so well that Augusta's grating question came as a shock. "And where, young man," demanded Augusta, rudely breaking into the conversation, "is your brother?"

Penelope looked at her in surprise and Charles flushed. "Roger will be here directly," he mumbled. "I promised you . . ."

Augusta became aware of Penelope's amazed stare and laughed shrilly. "The dear boy," she said, patting the Viscount on the cheek. "I'm like a mother to him, ain't I just?"

"How touching!" said a cold voice. "But Charles is out of short coats after all and does not, I think, need a substitute mother."

The Earl of Hestleton stood framed in the doorway. Penelope looked up and found he was staring straight across the room at her. He was a very tall man with a thin, white, high-nosed face and peculiarly light gray eyes, almost the color of silver, under heavy, drooping lids. His expression was austere and harsh, his hair an unusual copper color with red lights which glinted in the light from the chandeliers. He was dressed in a close-fitting black evening coat and black satin knee breeches with diamond buckles on his shoes. A magnificent diamond pin winked in the folds of his snowy cravat.

Penelope dismally decided that he was one of the most terrifying-looking men she had ever seen. She hurriedly cast down her eyes and studied the toe of her slipper.

The Viscount made the introductions. The Earl gave Miss Harvey a very slight bow and Penelope a lower one. She looked up once more into his eyes only to find her wide blue gaze trapped and held by that hard silvery stare.

Miss Harvey launched into speech and the Earl turned his gaze slightly from Penelope, but not so far away that she could not fail to observe his look of hauteur deepening to one of disgust.

"Naughty man," shrieked Miss Harvey coquetting awfully from her chair by the fire. "You don't think I'm like a mother to your little brother? Ah, but I am. I dote on the dear boy."

She lumbered to her feet and placed a fat arm around the horrified Viscount's neck and gave him an affectionate squeeze. He hurriedly rose to his feet to escape her embrace and fled to the corner of the room where he busied himself with the decanters.

"But you grand bucks are always teases," went on Miss Harvey, regardless, turning to the Earl who was still standing in front of Penelope. "You'll need to be careful, Penelope, my dear. This fine Lord eats hearts for breakfast, heh!"

"Pray be seated, madam," said the Earl icily. "I would be grateful if you could possibly modify the personal tone of your conversation. Tell me, Miss Vesey, are you recently come to London?"

But before Penelope could find her voice, Augusta rattled on. "Now, now, my lord. We musn't get twitty."

"Twitty?" said the Earl awfully. "Explain yourself, Miss Harvey."

"Mifty. Up in the boughs. Spleenish," said Augusta with a wide smile. "But don't mind me. I'm used to gentlemen and their little ways when they gets a twinge of the gout."

Pity for his brother made the Earl refrain from giving Augusta Harvey the terrible setdown he wished to. He contented himself for the moment by turning a deaf ear to her remarks.

The Earl decided Charles had been lying to him. His brother must obviously be smitten with Miss Vesey's undoubted beauty. He looked thoughtfully at Charles who blushed miserably and looked into his glass of wine.

He turned to concentrate his attention on

Penelope. But Penelope, ashamed of her aunt and overawed by the splendid Earl, muttered only brief replies to his questions. Yes, she had just arrived in London. Yes, she was enjoying herself. No, she had not yet been to the opera.

The Earl looked down thoughtfully at her bent head and wondered if the girl was as graceless as her aunt in a quieter way. The soft candlelight showed the perfection of Penelope's white skin and the silk dress displayed the soft curves of her slim figure to advantage. There was a vulnerability — a fragility — about her beauty that was infinitely feminine, decided the Earl.

He looked briefly across at Augusta Harvey and surprised a triumphant, gloating expression on that lady's face. His thin brows snapped together. Augusta could not — would dare not — look so high for a marriage partner for her niece! But that she hoped for some outcome from his interest in Penelope was all too obvious.

She is hoping I set the girl up as my mistress, thought the Earl, turning again to study Penelope. Perhaps it would be worth the vast amount of money he would probably have to pay Augusta. The girl was undoubtedly a diamond of the first water and, provided Penelope proved to be a willing partner in Augusta's plot, he might oblige. She looked like a lady, but appearances were obviously deceptive. Any filly out of Augusta Harvey's family stable would no doubt prove to be little better than a cart horse.

The Earl had been engaged, some ten years before, to a pretty little debutante, Lady Sarah Devane. He was charmed and fascinated by her kittenish ways and had fallen in love with her with all the fire and passion of his twenty-five years. Two weeks before the wedding he had called at her home unexpectedly. As the butler had been relieving him of his greatcoat in the hall, the silvery tones of his beloved in the drawing room had carried to his ears with deadly clarity. "Well, of course, Mama, I would much rather be marrying Bertram or someone like that. Roger is too *serious,*" Lady Sarah was saying. "But think of all Roger's *beautiful* money. And I shall enjoy being a Countess. Married ladies have such freedom . . ."

The Earl had covered his hurt and shock very well. He had quietly lied to Sarah's father that he had lost all his money on "Change" and felt it would be unfair to subject Sarah to an impoverished marriage. Sarah's father had heartily agreed. Sarah, too, had agreed with a pretty show of sighs and tears. By the time the Devanes had discovered his lie, Sarah was married to her Bertram. Since then the Earl had preferred to keep mistresses and flirt idly with several hopeful debutantes. And now, he mused as he looked at Penelope from under drooping lids, I am considering entangling myself with a young lady who has an aunt who is as common as a barber's chair.

Charles had begun to talk to Augusta in a high, nervous way about England's recent war with France and how marvellous it was that that monster Bonaparte was safely installed on Elba. He said all this with an almost pleading note in his voice, the Earl noted, and thought it was sad that young Charles so obviously did care quite a bit for Augusta's opinion.

Their mother had died when both the Earl and the Viscount were small boys. The Earl had not missed his mother much since he had seen little of her, having been brought up by a nanny and then a tutor before going to Eton. But perhaps, he reflected as Charles chattered on, his brother had felt the loss more than he, Roger, had ever imagined and was finding in the horrible Augusta a weird substitute.

Dinner was announced, and the Earl conducted Augusta into the dining room while Penelope and the Viscount trailed behind.

Unless one was a member of the Holland House set and accustomed to witty, garrulous, political dinner parties, one usually ate one's food at the tables of the best houses in a morbid silence. This dinner party was no exception. The Earl ate sparingly and seemed immersed in his thoughts, Charles was drinking steadily, Penelope was too overawed by the numerous footmen, the gold plate, and the formidable Earl to open her mouth, and only Augusta enlivened the silence by the steady chomping of her great jaws.

By the end of the meal the fact that Charles did not wish to remain alone with his brother became all too obvious when the port wine and walnuts were brought in. He started to rise to follow Augusta and Penelope, making some feeble joke about the ladies being too attractive to be neglected even for a moment.

"Sit down, Charles," said the Earl in a deceptively mild voice. "I am sure the ladies will forgive us for a few minutes."

Charles looked longingly after the retreating backs of Augusta and Penelope and slumped down sulkily in his chair.

"Now, Charles," said the Earl. "I must ask

you again what all this is about. I tell you now I will not have that infuriating woman across my threshold again. Tell me plain — does she hope I will offer her niece a *carte blanche?*"

"No!" said Charles. "Nothing like that." His sulkiness changed to petulant bad temper. "You're always twitting me about something, Roger. You're always so demned toplofty. So Miss Harvey is perhaps a bit of a rough diamond, but her niece is all that is proper."

"A proper niece would not be seen in the company of a woman like that," said the Earl coldly. "Pass the port, Charles, before you drink it all. Now tell me for once and for all — what do you see in a woman like Augusta Harvey?"

"She's kind to me, dammit," burst out Charles. "You always said this was my home as much as yours. Can't I invite my friends? You're always prosing on about something. It's like living with a demned Methodist preacher, that it is. I'll not stand for it."

"Very well," said the Earl, looking enigmatically at his brother from under his drooping lids. "You may entertain whom you will. But pray warn me next time Miss Harvey is expected, and I shall spend the evening at my club."

The Earl sighed and wondered if he were indeed being too harsh. But he had had to be both father and brother to Charles, who seemed to tumble into an endless succession of scrapes. He was constantly having to be rescued from one hell after another — where he was usually found dead drunk and with his pockets to let. His friends often belonged to the fringes of society but, to date, they had all been men. Thinking of Charles's friends, the Earl suddenly recollected something and frowned.

"I hear that the Comte de Chernier was staying at the Courtlands as a houseguest. I am surprised at the Courtlands giving house room to such a shady emigré. He has been seen in your company too. I would avoid that one, dear Charles. We may have ceased hostilities with France, but Bonaparte will never give up while he lives, and he is reported to have spies in London. The Comte must know that we have many friends in the higher echelons of the army."

Charles had turned paper white. "First you damn my lady friends and now you accuse a member of the French nobility of being a Bonapartiste spy. Well, let me tell you this, Roger, I shall choose my own friends and if you continue in this vein, I shall leave this house forever!"

"Think about what I have said," replied the Earl, looking at his brother sadly. "I am concerned for your welfare, Charles, that is all. There now. Let us say no more. Shall we join the . . . er . . . ladies?"

As soon as Penelope and Miss Harvey had been ushered into the drawing room, Penelope waited until the butler had retired and then turned and faced her aunt.

"I cannot go on with it," she said firmly while Augusta stared in amazement to see her niece so incensed. "Yes, I hope to find a husband this Season, but I will not prostitute myself, madam, in front of a sneering aristocrat who obviously thinks we are lower than the dirt beneath his feet. Oh, he noticed your winks and leers and smiles. I believe you have succeeded in convincing the Earl that I would suit as his mistress.

"I agreed to do the best I could, knowing nothing of the world, and thinking that such bold tactics, so repugnant to my nature, were the way of the world. But one look at the Earl's face and I knew they would not serve. I am aware I am entirely dependent on your charity, madam, but I will *not* humiliate myself in such a fashion!"

Penelope paused for breath, her cheeks flushed and her eyes blazing.

"Don't be in such a taking," said Miss Harvey, backing off a step. "You refine too much on things." Augusta thought furiously. She would love to turn this impertinent baggage out of doors, but the money she had already spent on the scheme should not — could not — go to waste so quickly.

She stretched her crocodile smile to its widest. "Perhaps I *was* too forward," she said with an awful laugh. "But, you see, I have your welfare at heart and was anxious to secure a good marriage for you. Forgive me, my dear. You can't blame me for wanting the best for you."

Penelope was immediately contrite. "I am sorry, Aunt, if I have been unjust. I shall try to do my best to please you — but fling myself at the feet of that . . . that . . . red-haired, white-faced Lord, I will not!"

"There, there," said Augusta. "Why don't you play a little something on the pianoforte, dear, and we won't say any more about it."

Penelope gratefully sat down on the music stool and began to play a piece by Scarlatti with exquisite precision, while Augusta plumped down in an armchair and thought furiously. Penelope was right. The Earl *had* looked disgusted. She had played her hand too quickly and too fast. She had thought that her wealth would have been enough to convince any Lord that his intentions toward her niece must be honorable, but that did not seem to be the case. Augusta reluctantly came to the conclusion that she must do something about herself first. She must somehow become more genteel. She furrowed her brow in concentration until the powder flaked down her face like dandruff.

Miss Stride, that was it! Miss Stride should teach Augusta Harvey how to behave like a Duchess. Then Augusta thought of the money the woman would demand and groaned.

Penelope played on, beginning to relax under the soothing spell of the music. She was extremely sorry she had berated her aunt and wondered what had come over her. Her aunt was not to blame for the Earl's attitude. Her aunt's manners *did* strike her as coarse, but the good woman was only trying to secure a future for her as any mother would. It was the Earl's *attitude* which had contrived to make poor Auntie seem vulgar. If he now believed she, Penelope, would be prepared to become his mistress, he was very much mistaken! Before this evening is out, thought Penelope, I shall make sure the noble Earl never wishes to set eyes on me again.

Augusta sat behind her, busily plotting

and planning. She was so engrossed in her thoughts that it was some time before she realised that Charles and his brother had entered the room. The Earl was sitting quite still, his long legs stretched out in front of him, listening to the music as it turned and rippled in its mathematical beauty round the elegant room.

Augusta roused herself to direct some social remark to the Earl, but he silenced her with a frown and sank back into his absorption of Penelope's playing.

Somewhere in Augusta's dark, feral, and tone-deaf soul, she realised that the Earl was enraptured. Hope sprang anew. I shall keep my mouth shut, she thought in surprise, and let things take their course.

While Charles fidgeted and worried and Augusta yawned and moved her bulk from one massive hip to the other, Penelope and the Earl sat lost in the world of music. All the Earl's worries about his brother fell away as he watched the slim, golden girl conjure magic out of the piano. Penelope herself was completely lost in the music, far away in the only refuge she had ever known.

When she struck the last chord, there was a little silence. Then the Earl rose to his feet and walked towards the pianoforte where Penelope sat, very still, with her motionless hands on the keys.

"That was exquisite, Miss Vesey," he said in a husky voice. "Beautiful playing by a beautiful performer. I pray you, will you sing for me?"

Penelope twisted slightly and looked up into his eyes. He was looking down at her, his gray eyes alight with warmth and a smile of singular sweetness lighting up his harsh features. She felt suddenly breathless and her body seemed to be undergoing a series of small physical shocks. She wanted to get away from him, to do something that would ensure this haughty Lord would not want to set eyes on her again. Penelope believed this sudden warmth and charm could only mean he planned to offer her his protection, but not his name.

"Very well, my lord," she said mildly.

The Earl bowed and returned to his seat.

Penelope ran her fingers lightly over the keys. She suddenly remembered a vulgar ballad her father's debauched friends used to sing when they were in their cups — so far gone they had forgotten there was a small girl in the room. What was it called? Ah . . . "The Harlot's Progress." Now, if that did not give my lord a disgust of her, then nothing would.

She began to play the deceptively simple

and jaunty introduction and then to sing the words in a clear, sweet voice.

"When Charlotte first increased the Cyprian corps,
She asked a hundred pounds — I gave her more,
Next year, to fifty sunk the course of trade:
I thought it now extravagant, but paid.
Six months elapsed, 'twas twenty guineas then,
In vain I prayed and press'd and proffer'd ten.
Another quarter barely flipp'd away,
She begged four guineas of me at the play:
I boggled — her demand still humbler grew,
'Twas 'thank you kindly, sir' for two pounds two.
Next, in the street, her favours I might win,
For a few shillings and a glass of gin.
— And now (though sad and wonderful it sounds)
I would not touch her for a hundred pounds."

Penelope rose quietly from the pianoforte, fully aware of the electric silence in the room behind her.

For once Augusta was at a loss for words. The Earl's face was a polite mask, and only Charles seemed to have trouble in concealing his emotions which eventually burst out in the form of a snigger which he quickly changed to a sneeze, burying his scarlet face in his handkerchief.

"Thank you," said the Earl coldly. "A most interesting choice of ballad. I hate to end our congenial party but the hour is late. . . ."

"Of course. Of course," said Augusta, desperate to escape. Drat the girl. She should be out in the street this very night. Baggage!

"Thank you for your company," said the Earl, bowing slightly over Augusta's trembling hand. He turned punctiliously to Penelope. "And, Miss Vesey, thank you for your performance. I regret I shall be very busy this Season so it is unlikely we shall meet again."

A small mischievous light danced somewhere in the back of Penelope's blue eyes and she said, "I am most certain we shall not meet again, my lord."

The Earl looked quickly down at her in sudden speculation. She had wanted him to take her in dislike. He was suddenly sure of it. He took her hand in his and looked down into her eyes, holding her gaze. "Of course, Miss Vesey, I should be loathe to lose the charming company of such an expert musician. Perhaps Miss Harvey would allow me to escort you this Thursday? A drive in the park, perhaps? You agree, Miss Harvey? Good. Until then, Miss Vesey."

He stood back and surveyed with satisfaction the look of alarm and dismay on Penelope's face while Augusta was still enthusiastically accepting the invitation on her behalf, over and over again. He had been right! It would be interesting to find out more about this Miss Vesey who could play like an angel, sing like a fallen one, and who was the only female in London who did not pine for the rich Earl of Hestleton's company!

Chapter Four

"Now," said Miss Stride in governess accents, "I am the Earl of Hestleton come to take Penelope driving. 'Good morning, Miss Harvey. I trust I find you well?' Now, you reply. Close your eyes and imagine I am Hestleton."

Augusta screwed up her eyes. "I'm doing very nicely, my lord," she said, "although I have a twinge of the old rheumatics in my hip. I take after my poor father what was a martyr to the rheumatics. I . . ."

"*Stop!*" Miss Stride held up her hand. "Miss Harvey. When someone asks you how you are, 'tis not necessary to tell them so with anatomical descriptions. Simply reply *on all occasions* that you are very well, thank you, and leave it at that. You will then offer him some refreshment — which he will decline — and after a genteel five minutes, you, Penelope, will make your entrance."

I wonder if I can go through with this, thought Miss Stride, looking at Augusta's fat and sulky features. Then she smoothed down her new gray velvet walking dress with a complacent hand. Augusta had indeed been generous. "*And*, Miss Harvey," pursued Miss Stride, "you must not wear so many bright colors and feathers. Outside of the ballroom, the *line* of an outfit is the thing, not the color. Now, shall we begin again? I am the Earl of Hestleton . . ."

Penelope sat at the window seat with her tambour frame and watched the comedy going on before her eyes with some amusement. It was the evening before the day on which she was to go driving with the Earl. Penelope had forgotten her fears of that gentleman and although she still felt he was a rather unnerving man, she decided that it was only a drive after all and she would probably not see him much after that.

She had forgotten the strange effect the Earl had had on her when he had smiled down at her when she sat on the piano stool. She had come to the conclusion that her own inexperience had overset her nerves that evening and that she had read sinister meanings and undertones into what had been probably quite innocent conversations.

The Viscount had called earlier in the day, very much the worse for wine, and had paid her vulgar and extravagant compliments which could have come from Augusta herself. Somehow his behavior had seemed to make the Hestletons less formidable and Augusta less outrageous by comparison.

Watching her aunt's struggles with the etiquette of receiving a call, Penelope could not help but be touched. She did not know of Augusta's plans to rise on the social ladder through her marriage and therefore thought that her aunt, despite her distressingly common ways, was showing a great degree of commendable and selfless generosity. That Augusta should try to turn herself into a lady, all for Penelope's sake, warmed that young girl's heart, and she felt guilty for all the hard thoughts she had previously nursed toward her aunt.

I must be a snob, after all, thought Penelope. How could I be so hard on poor Aunt simply because of her *gauche* behavior. Her heart is in the right place.

Augusta's heart at that moment was suffering under the humiliation of Miss Stride's lecture. It had taken a lot of bribery and pleading to get her to accept the job. Augusta eyed the plain, angular spinster sourly, wondering at the injustice of society. Miss Stride had hardly a penny to her name and yet was accepted everywhere, whereas she herself was wealthy and so far — apart from her visits to Hestleton and the Courtlands — had been unable to get a foot over any other aristocratic doorstep.

But she had her feeling of power to comfort her, power over the Earl's brother. And what was the name of that Frenchie Charles had been passing the papers to? The Comte de Chernier, that was it. One of the Courtlands' footmen had supplied her with the information. "When I have what I want out of the Viscount," thought Augusta, "I shall perhaps pay a visit to the Comte."

As she listened with half an ear to Miss Stride's lecture on correct topics for genteel conversation, Augusta looked thoughtfully across the room at her niece. Soft candle-light flickered over the gold curls of Penelope's hair. She looked as beautiful and as fragile as a piece of fine porcelain. Would her niece succeed in capturing the Earl's heart when so many others had failed?

She'd *better*, thought Augusta grimly, or out she goes.

Augusta suddenly realised that Miss Stride had changed the topic and had turned her hard gaze on the portraits of Augusta's "ancestors" lining the walls. "And those," Miss Stride was saying with a wave of her gloved hand, "must be put in the attic."

"My ancestors!" said Augusta in horror.

"Not *your* ancestors," said Miss Stride sweetly. "You bought those when young Emmens' home went under the hammer. *I* know it, and so will everyone else. You must replace them with some good landscapes and" she added hurriedly, seeing the look of fury on Augusta's face, "perhaps have your portrait painted. Yes, that's it, Miss Harvey. An elegant portrait of yourself above the fireplace would give the room tone."

That appealed immensely to Augusta's vanity, and she nodded her wigged head enthusiastically.

"And while we are on the subject of this room," went on Miss Stride. "Those glaring stripes do not go with the carpet. We cannot do anything about the stripes before tomorrow but *plain* curtains at the window, Miss Harvey, and do get rid of those cheap, tawdry, china ornaments. Haven't you anything else?"

"I've some nasty old China stuff in the attics," said Augusta sulkily. The Chinese vases and screens had belonged to her late employer and she had always found them depressing. "Probably Ming," said Miss Stride with a titter. "Really, Miss Harvey, it is just as well you have me to advise you."

"Is it?" said Augusta rudely. "I hope so. I

like my money's worth and I don't like to be cheated."

Penelope looked up quickly in surprise, and Augusta gave her a wide smile. Penelope smiled back. Of course, Aunt meant she hoped the vases were Ming, she thought, bending her head over her sewing again, and does not want to think she has been cheated with imitations. But for one awful moment, I actually thought she meant Miss Stride!

She then wondered what on earth the haughty Earl would think if he could see this frantic dress rehearsal for his call tomorrow.

As he prepared to ride over to Brook Street next day, the Earl wondered if he had taken leave of his senses. Miss Harvey's visit to the Courtlands' ball had left a wave of gossip washing about the clubs and salons of London, and, although she had not been seen at any function since then, society still mocked and talked.

The house in Brook Street, he had to admit as he rolled up in his high-sprung chaise, seemed very respectable. The brass knocker was well polished and the steps gleamed white.

A very correct butler ushered him into the hall and took his driving coat. Miss Harvey was modern enough to have her drawing room on the ground floor instead of the first, and the Earl was quickly announced.

At first he did not recognise Augusta in the respectable stout matron dressed in plum-colored silk of a discreet cut and wearing a large velvet turban. He asked her how she went on and waited cynically for a long and vulgar outburst. To his surprise, she only replied, "very well, thank you," and then went on to talk in subdued tones — pausing occasionally to correct her lapses in grammar — about the weather.

The peremptory little clock briskly snapped up five minutes of time and Penelope appeared. She was wearing a white muslin dress, high-waisted, with little puff sleeves edged with artificial honeysuckle which also decorated the deep flounces at the hem of her gown. Her sunny hair fell to her white shoulders in ringlets from under a bergère straw hat which framed her delicate features. She carried a fine Norfolk shawl over her shoulders and a pretty little chicken skin fan with ivory sticks in one gloved hand.

The Earl, decided Penelope, looked much more formidable than she had remembered, and her heart sank right down to the toes of her bronze kid Roman sandals.

He was wearing a blue coat with brass

buttons worn wide open over a transparent cambric shirt, rose waistcoat, and intricate cravat. Leather breeches and Hessian boots with jaunty little gold tassels completed the ensemble. His copper curls were intricately dressed in the Windswept, and one hard silver eye stared at her, horribly magnified, through the eye of his quizzing glass.

He let the glass fall and bent over her hand. "You are a vision of loveliness, Miss Vesey," he said with a slight mocking edge to his voice.

"I *am?*" declared Penelope, startled. She knew her blond good looks were decidedly unfashionable in a world which favored dark beauties. Then she realised the compliment was probably no more than a meaningless gallantry, and her face fell.

The Earl watched the various emotions chasing each other across her expressive face as he courteously held the door open for her. He was suddenly quite glad that he had decided to keep this appointment after all.

The Earl gave his full attention to his horses until he had maneuvered through the press of traffic and had entered the gates of Hyde Park. All at once it seemed as if the noise and bustle of London were left behind, and Penelope stared about her with delight at the cool stretches of green grass, the grazing cows and deer, and the huge old trees.

The Earl slowed his horses to a leisurely amble and then, turning to his companion asked, "And how are you enjoying your Season, Miss Vesey?"

"I am not really having a Season," said Penelope thoughtfully. "It seems that we are not considered quite fashionable enough. But I am enjoying the novelty of having pretty clothes and . . . oh . . . every sort of comfort."

"Are you not used to comfort?" asked the Earl, reining the carriage to a halt under the broad shade of an oak tree.

"Not really," said Penelope slowly. "Until recently I was an articled pupil at a seminary in Bath and, no, it was vastly *un*comfortable. But I would rather talk of pleasanter things. You must tell me about Almack's since it is highly unlikely that I shall ever be allowed past its hallowed portals."

The Earl looked down at her, quickly masking his surprise. Miss Vesey appeared to have no interest at all in attaching his affections. It was a novelty which should have been pleasant, but he felt strangely piqued.

He collected himself in order to reply to

her question. "Almack's, Miss Vesey, would not be rated above half were it not so exclusive. Everyone fights to get in and when they are there, they are blessed if they can see what all the fuss is about.

"The balls at Almack's are, as you no doubt know, held on Wednesdays. The lady patronesses are the Ladies Castlereigh, Jersey, Cowper, and Sefton, Mrs. Drummond Burrell, the Princess Esterhazy, and the Countess Lieven. Let me see — the most popular is Lady Cowper. Lady Jersey, on the contrary, goes on like a tragedy queen and while attempting the sublime, she frequently makes herself simply ridiculous. She is very rude and often illbred. Lady Sefton is kind, the Countess Lieven is haughty and exclusive, Princess Esterhazy is amiable, and Lady Castlereigh and Mrs. Burrell are very *grandes dames*. The female government of Almack's is sheer despotism, and they rule their gossiping, dancing world with a rod of iron."

"I believe the mazy waltz is being danced there," said Penelope. She had heard from the rich young misses of the Bath seminary that the waltz was a very *fast* dance indeed.

"It's catching on," said the Earl laconically. "But we have the celebrated Neil Gow from Edinburgh conducting the orchestra so we mostly still perform Scottish reels and English country dances. Ah, but I forgot. There is a *new* dance. It is called the quadrille and is danced by eight persons. In the first quadrille ever danced at Almack's, there was Lady Jersey, Lady Harriet Butler, Lady Susan Ryder, and Miss Montgomery. The men were the Count St. Aldegonde, Mr. Montgomery, Mr. Montague, and Charles Standish."

He paused and then said idly, "Would you care to go to Almack's, Miss Vesey?"

"Yes," said Penelope slowly. "Yes, I would. But it is not possible."

"Why?" asked the Earl abruptly. "Why do you wish to go to Almack's?"

Penelope sighed. He was being remarkably obtuse. "Why, my lord, does any female wish for a Season? Why does any young woman worth her salt wish to attend Almack's? To find a husband of course!"

"I have only known you a short time, Miss Vesey," said the Earl severely, "but somehow I would have thought you above the petty bartering of the marriage mart."

"Then what else do you suggest I do?" said Penelope reasonably. "A comfortable home of one's own is a better prospect than being employed as a drudge at some seminary. Besides, I should like children of my own. Marriage is the only career open to a lady in this day and age."

"And does love not enter into your calculations?" demanded the Earl with a hint of a sneer.

Penelope looked vaguely across the summer picture of the park. "Oh, love!" she said at last. "No, my lord, I have no money of my own. Love is a luxury I cannot afford."

She looked quickly up at his face and surprised the look of contempt in his eyes. "Why do you look *so?*" she demanded angrily. "It is easy for you to prate on about love, my lord. You have only to drop the handkerchief and any woman — with the exception of myself — would be glad to pick it up."

"So I do not enter into your marital plans?"

"No," said Penelope. "You are too high in the instep for me, my lord. Besides, you make me feel uncomfortable."

"In that case, Miss Vesey, you need not have come driving with me."

"Oh, but I had to," said Penelope simply. "Aunt Augusta would have been so disappointed. You see, she has brought me to London and has bought me oh! so many beautiful clothes. She was very flattered by your invitation to dinner. It would have been cruel to disappoint her. I am being un-fashionably honest with you, my lord, be-cause I am sure there are so many other females who would enjoy your company im-mensely and it is not necessary to waste your time with me. I believe you are consid-ered quite handsome," she added in a kind voice.

"My fortune certainly is, and where my fortune leads, my face must follow," he said dryly. "Tell me, Miss Vesey, did you sing that singularly naughty ballad the other night in order to disgust me?"

"Yes," said Penelope with an infectious ripple of laughter. "Was it not dreadful? Papa's friends were six-bottle-a-day men, you know, and would often sing it when they were in their cups and too far gone to notice a little girl in the corner of the room."

"Your father?" The Earl frowned. "Was he by any chance a relation of Sir James Vesey?"

"His youngest son."

"But good God, girl, the Vesey family would supply you with all the entrée you need!"

"My father was considered to have mar-ried beneath him," said Penelope quietly. "Sir James took a dislike to Aunt Augusta in particular. He has shown no interest in me."

The Earl fell silent. It was certainly not unusual on the part of Sir James in a world where people often cut their own mothers and fathers socially if they considered them not fashionable enough.

Penelope looked so calm and assured as she sat sedately behind him. He felt she should have at least made some fashionable effort to flirt. He suddenly wanted to make a crack in that beautiful and porcelain composure.

He turned and leaned towards her. "But have you considered what any marriage would be like to a man you did not love?"

"Of course," said Penelope, resolutely banishing her adolescent dreams of a strong and handsome lover. "I should not see much of him at all, you see. If gentlemen are not at their clubs or their politics, they are on the hunting field."

"Ah, but were I in love with someone," said the Earl, forcing her to meet his gaze, "I would not leave her side for a moment."

Penelope felt suddenly breathless and awkward. She rapidly held her fan in front of her face. "Since we shall not be seeing *anything* of each other in the future, my lord, we should not be talking like this."

The Earl studied the top of her frivolous hat as she bent her head and lowered her fan to her lap and stared at its painted pictures.

"Jobbins!" said the Earl, without removing his gaze from Penelope. "There is a fine oak tree about a hundred yards to your left. Go and count the branches."

"Very good, my lord," said his groom, Jobbins, with a grin, and climbed down from his perch.

The Earl waited a few moments and then asked gently. "Do you know why I sent Jobbins away, Miss Vesey?"

"No," said Penelope in a small voice.

"Because I wish to kiss you."

"Oh!"

"Is that all you can say?" teased the Earl. " 'Oh.' "

"I appeal to you as a gentleman," said Penelope primly, "not to take advantage of our isolated position." Their quarter of the park was deserted, the fashionable throng having made their way to parade their carriages in the Ring.

"But I am about to take advantage of our isolated position," the infuriating, teasing voice went on.

Penelope sighed. "Oh, go ahead. I am not going to make a cake of myself by fleeing across Hyde Park on foot." She shut her eyes and screwed up her face. He looked down at her for a second in some amusement and then took her very gently in his arms. He kissed her eyelids and the tip of her small straight nose, and then his wandering mouth suddenly clamped down over her own. Penelope's last coherent thought before she was carried away on a buffeting sea of emotions, and tremblings and strange, tortured virginal passions was that Sir James Vesey might have had some point in thinking they were a vulgar family. No lady would behave so. No lady would feel so.

At last he raised his head and the world of sunlight and trees and grass came swirling back. She looked up into his eyes and found them as hard and cold as the winter sea. Why should he look at her like that? It was his fault after all.

The Earl brusquely summoned his groom and set his horses in motion. "We shall join the fashionables, Miss Vesey," he said coldly, "and then I shall take you home."

Roger, Earl of Hestleton, was furious. The girl had succeeded in awaking a series of emotions he had considered long dead and buried. Had Penelope made some flirtatious remark, he would have snapped her head off. But she sat very quiet and still and rather white-faced. He slowly became aware that he had behaved very badly indeed and set himself to make amends.

As they joined the series of glittering carriages in the Ring, he asked lightly, "Well, Miss Vesey, here we have the cream of society. What do you think?"

Penelope looked about her, wide-eyed, her recent distress temporarily forgotten. It was a glittering spectacle as the dandies and their ladies promenaded to display their elaborate toilettes and spanking carriages pulled by the finest horses. Many ladies were driven in a little carriage for two persons, called a vis-à-vis. This gorgeous equipage had a hammer cloth, rich in heraldic designs, powdered footmen in smart liveries, and a coachman who looked as stately as an archbishop. Then she laughed, "I feel like a poor child looking in the window of a pastry cook's. I suppose I shall always be outside, looking in."

"Would you like to attend Almack's?" asked the Earl abruptly.

"You have already asked me that question," said Penelope patiently.

"I mean — *really* attend."

"Of course."

"I can arrange it," he said simply.

Penelope looked at him, wide-eyed. "How?"

"Like this," he said with a charming smile

lighting up his austere face. He inched his carriage forward and then began to introduce Penelope to various notables. Names and titles flew about her bewildered ears, hard eyes stared and speculated, jealous female eyes flicked back and forth from the Earl's face to her own, dandies bowed and simpered, Corinthians stared and leered.

Obviously the Earl of Hestleton had great social power. When it was discovered she was Augusta Harvey's niece, though it caused some rapid blinking, it did not seem to make much difference to the polite, if formal, reception given to her by the fashionable set. If the Earl of Hestleton found nothing to disgust him in Augusta Harvey, then neither would they. From being a vulgar, pushing mushroom, Augusta was elevated in their minds to the rank of a tedious eccentric, and after all, there was always some new butt around to receive the barbed attention of society.

Penelope was then introduced to two of the patronesses of Almack's and, luckily for her, to two of the most amiable, Lady Sefton and Lady Cowper. Both patronesses decided that Penelope's behavior was unexceptionable and allowed that she was quite pretty although it was a pity she was so unfashionably fair.

The Earl's suggestion that vouchers for Almack's should be sent to Penelope was met with a pleasant "perhaps" instead of the open horror which would have met such a request had it been made by any other. Such are the fickle vagaries of fashion.

As they drove from the park, Penelope had forgotten her desire to be free of the Earl's company and turned a glowing face up to his. "Oh, *thank* you," she breathed.

" 'Tis nothing," he said, looking down briefly at the enchanting face turned up towards his. "It will all be worth it to see Miss Harvey's debut at Almack's."

Penelope bit her lip. He had not really been kind. Only indulging in a fit of whimsy. And the kiss, the memory of which still made her feel weak, had meant nothing to him.

She sat in silence until he deposited her in Brook Street. She must marshal her wayward thoughts and take full opportunity of her new social status and find a husband. Some kindly country squire would suit admirably.

Chapter Five

"You *must not* fidget, madam," said the artist, Mr. Liwoski.

Augusta gave him a sulky glare. She was paying him for his services, wasn't she? But Miss Stride had said that Mr. Liwoski was the best and cheapest that Soho could provide, and since Penelope was in the room, she contented herself by turning her eyes to the card rack on the mantelpiece where two vouchers to Almack's were prominently displayed.

It had been like a dream come true. Penelope had said shyly that it was because of the kindness of the Earl of Hestleton, but Miss Augusta Harvey had put it down to her own new genteel image and, of course, the wily Miss Stride had encouraged her in that idea.

Penelope sat silently on her favorite corner of the window seat, content to watch Mr. Liwoski at work. A day or so ago he had completed a series of quick thumbnail sketches and was now starting on his canvas, laying down the ground surface of thin wash, a "brown sauce" he called it. He then occasionally wiped it with a rag to bring out the masses of light on the brow and the cheekbone, carefully checking the likeness from time to time. He had told the fascinated Penelope that a difference of quarter of an inch in the brushstroke, say on the lips, could make a mouth sinister or cruel if one were not very careful.

He was a thin, threadbare young man, who perpetually looked in need of a good meal which was, in fact, often the case.

Penelope watched his deft expert movements and dreamed of the evening at Almack's to come.

She had taken dancing lessons in the art of performing the quadrille and the waltz. That very evening she would walk through the doors of Almack's. She wondered if the Earl would be there. Try as she would, she could not forget that kiss. She should not have responded to it. But then the Earl should not have kissed her in the first place. Maybe he knew his advances would not be rejected, thought poor Penelope with scarlet cheeks.

His brother, Charles, had already engaged her for the first dance. He was vastly different from his austere brother, reflected Penelope. He was a frequent caller and always seemed to treat Aunt Augusta with a mixture of flattery and fear.

It was indeed very strange. But the behavior of so many people in London seemed strange. The famous dandies were not the elegant gentlemen that Penelope had been led to believe. She had already seen many of them as they sauntered down Piccadilly and Bond Street. There seemed to be nothing remarkable about them but their insolence. Generally middle-aged, with rude, ill-bred manners, they were neither good looking, nor clever, nor agreeable. They swore a good deal, never laughed, and had their own particular brand of slang. The sportsmen, the Corinthians, seemed just as bad. Where the dandies minced, they swaggered and although their oaths were the same, they were pronounced in louder voices.

The young men, like Charles, who tried to ape the dandy set unfortunately copied their bad manners and their ridiculously exaggerated dress. The Earl, decided Penelope, could not be a dandy. He was too well-dressed. He could turn his head in the high confines of his cravat, and his coats were not tailored so that his collars bunched halfway up the back of his head.

Penelope became aware that Mr. Liwoski was packing up his materials. "After I have completed your portrait, madam," he said to Miss Harvey, "I would be grateful if you would commission me to paint your lovely niece's portrait."

"Humph! We'll see," was all Augusta would say. She looked at Penelope and cast a meaning look at the clock. Penelope rose obediently to her feet. It would take the rest of the day to prepare for the all-important evening ahead.

To the Earl's world-weary eyes Almack's may have seemed dull, but to Penelope's it appeared the epitome of high fashion. She felt like Cinderella arriving at the ball. Jewels flashed their myriad lights under the sparkling prisms of the crystal chandeliers. The air was heavy with scent worn by the guests, male and female alike, beeswax polish, oil lamps, and flowers. The dancers were whirling energetically in a Scottish reel, long tails flying, feathers bouncing as they weaved their way through the patterns of the figure eight.

The music stopped and Penelope found the Viscount at her side. He was correctly dressed in black and white. His cravat was snowy perfection and his knee breeches and stockings clung to his coltish legs without a wrinkle. He led her towards a set for a country dance that was just being made up and whispered in her ear, "I say, Miss Vesey. You look stunning. Take all the shine out of the others. By Jove, indeed you do!"

Penelope laughed at his gallantry, well aware that she could not possibly compete with any of the dark beauties with their intricate masses of brown or black hair and their flashing jewels. She did not know that the Viscount had spoken only the truth.

Her blond hair was dressed high on her head in a mass of soft curls with one thick ringlet falling onto her shoulder. Her dress was of the finest white Indian muslin, threaded under the breast with gold ribbons. The neckline was fashionably low and was framed by a stiffened lace collar, pointed in the Elizabethan manner. Her only ornaments were the modest string of pearls at her throat and a thin pearl and gold circlet set among her curls.

When the figure of the dance briefly brought Penelope and her partner together, the Viscount suddenly whispered to her, "Have a care! You are too young and innocent to have an aunt like that!"

Penelope flushed with anger and, when

their steps brought them together again, she said, "If you dislike my aunt so much, why do you keep calling on us?"

"Because of you, my dear," said Charles with one of the falsest smiles Penelope thought she had ever seen.

Penelope bit her lip as she gracefully twisted and turned in the steps of the dance. She could not see the Earl anywhere. Almack's was not such a splendid place, after all!

The dance ended. Then the quadrille was announced, and Penelope found herself without a partner.

From her vantage point beside Miss Harvey's great bulk, Miss Stride noted the fact and whispered to her companion, "It is generally known that your niece has no money."

"So," said Augusta. "What are you trying to say? Stop mumbling and get to the point." Augusta did not waste any of her newfound airs and graces on Miss Stride.

"Well, if a girl is portionless, she is apt to lack dancing partners. Even rich men fight shy of a dowerless girl. You should let me put it about that you will leave Penelope your fortune when you die and *then* you will see the men flutter about her."

"I ain't leaving her a penny," snapped Augusta.

"Really!" replied Miss Stride acidly. "What *were* you going to do with your money when you died. Take it with you?"

Augusta had not once thought of death. That was something that happened to other people. But it would do no harm to *say* she was leaving the girl her money. "Oh, very well," she said sourly, "though I must say I'm surprised that these society gents should be so mercenary."

"Gentlemen," corrected Miss Stride automatically and wondered why Augusta, so mercenary herself, should be so surprised to discover other people to be the same. But then one always intensely dislikes the faults in other people that one has oneself.

Miss Stride rose to her feet and began to drift from group to group, whispering and chattering, her feathered headdress bobbing and nodding. She looked for all the world like an elderly chicken scratching for grain.

Penelope was watching the quadrille since she had never seen it performed except by her dancing master. One lady was performing her steps with marvellous expertise. She learned later that the expert was none other than the beautiful Lady Harriet Butler who had received dancing lessons from the celebrated Vestris. She was making the most beautiful *entrechats*, leaping from the floor and beating her little feet in the air to the amazement and admiration of a watching audience. She was partnered by the fat and elderly Lord Graves who was so overcome by his fair partner's *entrechats* that he attempted to do the same. He leaped up in the air and then fell heavily on the floor. Poor Lord Graves staggered to his feet and performed the rest of the dance as best he could.

When the quadrille finished, Lord Graves and Lady Harriet were just passing Penelope, when Lord Graves was waylaid by Sir John Burke, who said in a very sarcastic voice, "What induced you at your age and in your state to make so great a fool of yourself as to attempt an *entrechat?*"

Lord Graves faced Sir John, his large face empurpled with fury. "If you think I am too old to dance," he snapped, "I consider myself not too old to blow your brains out for your impertinence. So the sooner you find a second the better."

Penelope held her breath. Was this going to result in a duel? But Lord Sefton had heard the discussion and came quickly to the rescue. He put a slim hand on the enraged Lord Graves's arm. "Tut, tut, tut, man," he said soothingly, "the sooner you shake hands the better, for the fact is, the world will condemn you both if you fight on such slight grounds. And you, Graves, won't have a *leg* to stand on."

Lord Graves and Sir John burst out laughing and shook hands, and Penelope, turning round, saw that she was being surrounded by men, begging for the next dance. Miss Stride had done her work well. No one wanted Miss Harvey with her seventy-five thousand pounds. But the beautiful Penelope with that amount of money was a different matter.

And so that was how the Earl of Hestleton saw her when he entered the ballroom at Almack's. She was laughing and blushing, her large blue eyes sparkling with delight, surrounded by her court of admirers.

I have indeed helped Miss Penelope well on the road to matrimony, thought the Earl wryly. He was irked to discover that Penelope was so sought after. He realised that he had believed the vulgarity of her aunt and her own lack of fortune would have prevented such popularity. He had envisaged her sitting quietly on her rout chair at Almack's, perhaps dancing with Charles, but certainly awaiting his arrival anxiously. With a feeling of pique he realised she had not even noticed him entering the room.

He leaned against a pillar under the musicians gallery and, as Neil Gow and his orchestra sawed away enthusiastically at yet another Scottish reel, he was able to observe the grace and elegance with which Miss Vesey performed her steps.

"I'm paying her too much attention," he thought and turned his gaze elsewhere. His pale eyes narrowed as he saw his brother entering the cardroom on the far side with the Comte de Chernier. He detached himself from the pillar and made his way round the ballroom in pursuit of them, unaware that Penelope was watching him go and wondering why she felt so flat.

The Comte de Chernier and Charles were standing in a corner of the cardroom, talking quietly. The Comte was dressed in the finest elegance. His hair was powdered and his evening dress sparkled with jewels. He had a thin yellowish face and black eyes which did not seem to register any emotion at all. As the Earl watched, Charles cautiously drew some papers out of his pocket and slipped them to the Comte.

The Earl strode across the room and towered over them. His thin, strong hand clasped the Comte's ruffled wrist. "Have you been gambling, Charles?" he demanded. Both Charles and the Comte were staring down at the Earl's hand as if mesmerised. Then the Comte gave a light laugh and said, "I see I have been found out. These are unfortunately some love letters of mine. Charles was my messenger of love and took them to the lady but . . . alas . . ." His shoulders rose and fell in a Gallic shrug. "She returned them, as you see."

"And what the hell has it got to do with you, Roger?" gritted Charles, his pallor highlighting the marks of dissipation on his young face. "Were you not my brother, I would call you out!"

The Earl released the Comte's wrist, but his eyes still seemed to bore into the package of papers. "Please accept my apologies, Monsieur le Comte. I am . . . er . . . overprotective where my brother is concerned."

"Very commendable," drawled the Comte, shaking out his ruffles. "I gather you thought Charles was giving me his note of hand."

"Precisely," said the Earl. "You see it has happened before. But you have given me your word, Charles, that you have ceased gambling and it is monstrous of me not to take you at your word. Come, little brother, shake hands with me and say you forgive me."

Charles glared at him and then felt the Comte prod him urgently in the back. "Oh, very well," he said ungraciously. "But mind you don't do it again. You ain't my father, you know."

"No," said the Earl with a sigh, "I'm not — although I sometimes think it would be easier an' I were."

The Earl bowed to the Comte, nodded to his brother, and turned on his heel and walked back into the ballroom. A frown of worry creased his brow. Charles had been lying, of that he was sure.

Charles drew a breath of relief and then turned to his companion. "Look, de Chernier," he said. "I can't stand much more of this. I snitched these papers from Horseguards when I was visiting old Colonel Witherspoon. And I've been thinking. You can't expose me without exposing yourself. What if I tell Roger everything?"

"Then you will hang," said the Comte, "and so will I. But think, dear boy, my work here is nearly finished. Two more months and then you shall be free."

"I can't go on," said Charles, his thin face working with emotion. "I'm a traitor to my country. Do you know what that means, damn you!"

"Keep your voice down," said the Comte smoothly. He produced a roll of bank notes from his pocket and held them up in front of

Charles who stared at the money as if hypnotised. "Payment for services rendered," said the Comte softly.

"I won't take it," said Charles wildly. "At least you will no longer be able to say I took the money."

"At Watier's this evening," said the Comte, still holding the money in front of Charles's face, "there is a game of hazard. Golden Ball is playing." "Ball" Hughes was reputed to be the richest man in London.

"No," gasped Charles. "I won't." But already the gambling fever was burning in his eyes.

"Think," went on the Comte, leaning his thin face close to the Viscount. "If you pay me back, all I have given you, then I shall return you the papers and you will be free."

"You swear it," gasped Charles.

"My word as a de Chernier," said the Comte with a smile.

"I'll take it, God damn your rotten soul," said Charles. "I know I shall be lucky tonight." He tore the money from the Comte's hand and almost ran from the room.

The Comte brushed his fingers lightly and turned to enter the ballroom. He found his way was blocked by a large lady with a smile like an alligator.

" 'Scuse me, dear Comte," said this apparition, "being so forward and all. But I am a friend of the Hestletons. Miss Augusta Harvey is my name. Feel free to call on me anytime you wish. I know. . . ."

But the Comte rudely pushed past her without a word, and Augusta watched him go with an unlovely smile on her face which changed to one of real delight. Penelope was waltzing with the Earl.

Penelope had danced every dance except the waltz since she had not been given permission by the Patronesses to dance it and none of her partners had been enterprising enough to request that permission. It was the Earl who had prevailed on Lady Cowper to allow Penelope to stand up with him.

He now held her in his arms and looked down at her flushed and happy face. "You look so beautiful, Miss Vesey," he whispered, "that I am sorely tempted to kiss you again."

"Oh, how *can* you," cried Penelope with flaming cheeks.

"Quite easily," he teased. "But not at Almack's. I should never live it down."

"I-I d-do not want y-you to think I l-let gentlemen kiss me," stammered Penelope. "I had never been kissed before."

"Let me assure you," replied the Earl earnestly, "that you do it *very* well."

"Oooooh!" breathed Penelope. "How *in-*

furiating you are! You obviously think I am not a lady."

"On the contrary," he said in a husky voice, "I find you *adorable*."

Penelope glanced swiftly up into his eyes, and the warmth and intensity of his gaze nearly stopped her heart.

The dance came to an end, and Penelope's next partner immediately appeared. She stared back at the Earl with an almost pleading look on her face, and he gave her a reassuring smile.

The Earl had tumbled suddenly and irrevocably into love. When he had held her in his arms during the first bars of the waltz, he had realised with a shock of alarm that he never wanted to let go of her again. He thought wildly of what he owed his ancient name, he thought of Augusta Harvey — and all in vain. He wanted Penelope Vesey as his wife.

Chapter Six

Despite the Earl's social power, not all of polite society rushed to leave cards at the house in Brook Street. But a few did arrive, and that was a beginning as far as Augusta Harvey was concerned.

Her daily lessons from Miss Stride continued and did much to modify her dress and manner although she could only sustain the latter improvement for very short periods indeed.

Mr. Liwoski worked diligently on Augusta's portrait, and Penelope sat on the window seat and alternately watched him and dreamed of the Earl.

She had not seen him since that ball at Almack's. Three long days had passed and still he did not call. She tried to put him down in her mind as an accomplished flirt and then remembered the warm expression in his eyes and was slightly comforted.

The Prince Regent had held a tremendous dinner at Clarence House in honor of the visiting French royal family the day before. Neither Augusta nor her niece had been invited. *That* was aiming too high, too soon, Miss Stride had informed them with a superior air.

Clarence House and its grounds had been thrown open that day to the curious public, and Augusta had had to be almost forcibly restrained from going. Only the common people would be there, Miss Stride had assured her.

Charles had not called either. Rumors were flying about London that he had won a vast amount at Waiter's. Penelope, who had guessed that Charles suffered from the Fatal Curse, wondered if concern for his young brother had kept the Earl away.

The Earl had in fact been called away to his estates on urgent business and had therefore not heard of his brother's gambling success.

Charles at that moment was triumphantly rapping on the Courtlands' knocker. He had gone to settle his debt with the Comte. Yes, the Comte de Chernier was at home and would be pleased to see him, he was informed, and Charles took a deep breath of relief. The nightmare would soon be over.

The Comte was not yet dressed and was

wearing a magnificent brocaded dressing gown. He turned with a smile of welcome when Charles was announced which faded when he saw the triumphant smile on the other's face.

Charles waited impatiently until the footman had withdrawn and then said, "The day of reckoning has come, my dear de Chernier. I am here to pay back every penny I owe you!"

"Nonsense, dear boy," said the Comte, cleaning his nails with an orange stick, "I would not dream of taking it from you."

"*What!*" The smile was wiped from Charles's face. "But you gave your word. You gave your word as a de Chernier."

"So I did," said the Comte languidly, "and I hope the de Cherniers appreciate it — or their headless ghosts rather. If I have it right, the complete line of de Chernier died out under the guillotine."

"You are an impostor," said Charles, his face turning ashen.

"That, yes, and a few other things too tedious to mention," said the Comte, throwing down the orange stick and standing up.

"What is your real name?"

"None of your business, dear Charles. Come now! Enact me no Haymarket tragedies. This is real life. What is a country after all? What is patriotism? A myth. I work for money and so should you."

Charles thrust his hand into the pocket of his frock coat and drew out a pistol which he pointed at the Comte's head with a trembling hand.

"Oh, go ahead and blow my brains out if you must," sneered the Comte. "But my papers will be examined after my death and your name is mentioned in them. Believe me. It is very much to your interest to keep me alive. Come now, only two months and you will be free."

Charles let the pistol fall and sank into a chair with a groan and buried his head in his hands. "Two months! I don't think I can live through another hour of it."

"You will, you will," said the Comte indifferently. "And now, dear boy, this is what I want you to do . . ."

"If my brother ever finds out," interrupted Charles, beginning to cry in a hopeless, dreary way, "he'll kill me. Anyway, Augusta Harvey knows about it. She was hiding behind that screen on the night of the Courtlands' ball and heard every word."

The Comte's eyes narrowed into slits, and he crossed the room in a few quick strides and shook the sobbing Charles until his teeth rattled. "She has been blackmailing you, yes? What does she want?"

"She wants Roger to marry her niece. She wants to be accepted by society."

"*Vraiment!* And that is all this woman demands in return for her silence?"

"Yes," said Charles sulkily, wiping his streaming eyes on his sleeve.

"Then I shall call on her," said the Comte softly. "She is dangerous . . . and must be removed."

Penelope and Miss Harvey had been invited to a party to be given at a Mrs. Skeffington's villa that very evening. The villa was some way out of town on the Richmond Road with beautiful stretches of formal gardens running down to the brown and gray waters of the Thames.

It was a glorious evening when they arrived accompanied by Miss Stride. The air was very still and sweet and heavy with the scents of summer. A Viennese orchestra was playing waltzes under the trees, and a blackbird, silhouetted against the pale green sky, added a glorious counterpoint to the lilting music.

Penelope found herself trembling with anticipation. Perhaps *he* would be there. But one by one the guests arrived, and there was no sign of the tall figure of the Earl. She began to feel sad. Augusta was noisily and resentfully drinking tea, Miss Stride having forbidden her to touch anything stronger. Port wine had a nasty habit of bringing all Augusta's horrible manners to the surface.

"If you sit there all night with a long face, nobody's going to look at you," said Augusta sourly to Penelope. "What is more, God will never forgive you for passing up your opportunities. He's like that, you know. He strikes the sinner with a bolt of lightning from on high. Don't ever forget it, Penelope. I don't," she added moodily, alternately picking her teeth with a tired goose quill and slurping her tea.

"Miss Vesey?" said a tentative voice at Penelope's ear. She looked up and saw a stocky young man with a pleasant tanned face and merry blue eyes.

"Allow me to introduce myself," he went on. "The name's Manton, Guy Manton, friend of Hestleton. Roger's coming along later, but he asked me to take care of you. They are making up a set for the quadrille, and I wondered if you would grant me the honor of a dance, Miss Vesey?"

Penelope's heart soared like the song of the blackbird. The Earl had not forgotten her. He had sent this charming young man to look after her and . . . wonder upon wonder . . . he would be here in person later.

She smiled her assent and rose gracefully from her seat and allowed Mr. Manton to escort her towards a marquee in the garden which had been turned into a flower-bedecked ballroom.

Augusta had fastened her gooseberry cycs on the large ruby winking in Mr. Manton's stock and had given her assent with her eyes still fixed steadily on the jewel as if she were allowing the ruby rather than the wearer permission to take Penelope into the ball-room.

Mr. Manton danced the quadrille with more enthusiasm than finesse and made Penelope laugh, when the musicians struck the last chord, by saying he was glad the awful dance was over. "The quadrille's more suitable for a caper merchant than a gentleman," he said roundly. "But let me get you some refreshment, Miss Vesey."

He led Penelope towards another mar-quee which contained a long buffet and a se-ries of little tables. Unfortunately Augusta had not only found the buffet but the port wine as well. Port was drunk with every-thing, most of society still considering such wines as Burgundy and claret "wishy-washy stuff." She came waddling up to them with her protruding eyes slightly glazed.

"Ah, Mr. Manton," she smiled while her busy brain turned over the information she had received from Miss Stride — Guy Manton, country squire and soldier, comfortable income but nothing near as much as the Earl. "So you have been looking after my little Penelope. Pretty little thing, ain't she. All the bucks is mad about her, ain't they, my duckie?" Here she pinched Penelope's cheek. "Why, even the Earl of Hestleton had taken such a fancy to her as never was. It's the good Lord looking after the orphan, that it is. Although she owes everything to her auntie and she'll never forget it for she don't want to be struck dead from on high. People don't, you know."

Penelope's face flamed crimson with embarrassment. Her aunt's subdued behavior of the last few days seemed to have miraculously disappeared.

Mr. Manton was surveying Miss Harvey with amusement. "That's a good Christian spirit you have there, ma'am," he said gleefully. "I gather you believe strongly in divine punishment."

"Of course I does," said Augusta earnestly. "Do you know what happens to you when you go to hell?" She lowered her voice to a whisper.

"She's mad," thought Penelope wildly.

She's glorious, thought Mr. Manton. Funniest old quiz I've met in years. "Go on, Miss Harvey," he said out loud. "Do tell us all about it."

"It's like this," said Augusta, moving close to Mr. Manton. "When you die, like, if you've been a sinner, they takes away all your clothes, the demons do, so you're all naked. Then they lead you to the edge of this pit and down below it's all fire and brimstone. Then they takes their pitchforks and they shoves them right up —"

"Miss Harvey!"

Augusta turned round sulkily and then looked like a guilty child as she met the blazing eyes of Miss Stride. Having now some money in the bank had brought out all Miss Stride's latent and forceful personality, and Augusta, like all bullies, cringed before a stronger character.

"Miss Harvey," said Miss Stride again in a very governess sort of voice, "I wish you to accompany me. You have not yet been introduced to Lady Skeffington."

Rather in the manner of a jailer, Miss Stride led Augusta away.

Mr. Manton looked helplessly at Penelope. He tried to speak but could only manage a few choked sounds. Finally he gasped, "Excuse me, Miss Vesey," and fled out into the garden.

The Earl of Hestleton, who had entered the Skeffington's estate by a side entrance, paused in amazement. The most dreadful choking sounds were coming from behind a clump of rosebushes.

He peered round and found his friend, Guy Manton, doubled up in a paroxysm of laughter. Tears streamed down his face, and he chortled and gasped and snorted.

"Control yourself, Guy," said the Earl, much amused. "What is the reason for all this mirth? Have the Skeffingtons hired Grimaldi for the evening?"

He had to wait several minutes before his friend could compose himself enough to reply.

"It's that Harvey woman," said Guy when he could. He told the Earl about Miss Harvey's vision of hell, but the Earl was not amused.

"And you left Penelope standing alone," said the Earl crossly. "I had better go and look after her."

He strode off, leaving his friend to look after him in some amazement. Roger could not possibly be serious about the pretty Penelope. The girl was well enough but — oh, my stars — the aunt!

The Earl was thinking much the same as

he went in search of Penelope. He could not possibly marry the girl! There was a certain amount, after all, that he owed to his name.

Penelope was not beside the buffet, nor was she in the ballroom. He diligently searched the house and gardens and at last, under the light of an enormous full moon, saw her sitting in a dark corner of the garden on a rustic bench. He could make out the pale aura of her hair.

He felt a little wrench at his heart as he leaned over her and saw that she was crying. He sat down beside her and gently drew her hands away from her face. He found himself murmuring silly nothings, the way one does to a hurt child. "There, there. Come now, silly little puss. What a fuss! Dry your eyes and tell me all about it."

The fact that the stern Earl was talking to her in such a kind way helped to dry Penelope's tears.

"Now," he said, kissing her forehead, "what's all this about?"

"I feel so silly," wailed Penelope. "I can't tell you."

"I am your friend, Penelope," said the Earl, using her Christian name for the first time. "Tell me."

Penelope stared miserably at the toes of her slippers. How could she explain her muddled feelings about her aunt? Augusta often seemed like a summer's day when a storm is approaching: serene and sunny calm with gathering black clouds of suspected cruelty lit with sudden lightning flashes of pure madness.

"It's . . . it's just that I am so ashamed of being ashamed of her," said Penelope at last in a low voice. "I feel so disloyal. Mr. Manton was escorting me to the buffet and Aunt started talking some awful nonsense about hell and it made me miserable to hear her talking so wildly — so strangely."

The Earl bit his lip. He longed to tell Penelope that he was sure Augusta Harvey was using her beautiful niece as a sort of calling card on the best houses but did not want to hurt her feelings. Instead he said gently, "Miss Harvey is a trifle eccentric, that is all. London is full of such eccentrics and no one thinks them strange. Also, you have *my* social patronage. I promised you."

"You only promised me vouchers to Almack's," said Penelope, suddenly shy. "I was afraid I would not see you again."

"I had to go to my estates. There was trouble with one of the tenant farmers. How else could I leave you?"

Penelope's heart began to beat very quickly indeed, and she looked shyly up into his face; it was in the shadow as his back was to the moonlight. "I cannot see your face," she whispered.

"Can you feel my lips?" he asked, bending slowly towards her until his head blotted out the moon and his warm lips closed on hers and all the world went flying away leaving her alone on a black plain of passion, held closely in the Earl's arms.

They kissed with increasing ardor, Penelope innocently matching passion for passion, until he slipped her low gown from her shoulders and bent his mouth to her breasts and she began to tremble in his arms. "I go too fast, my darling," he murmured, releasing her. "I must endeavor to wait until we are married." He gently pulled her gown back on her shoulders.

"You will marry me, Penelope," he said.

"With all my heart," said Penelope softly.

"Then we shall announce our engagement," he said. "Our very short engagement."

But, oh Lord, thought the Earl as he led Penelope back towards the house. *How Augusta Harvey will gloat!*

Chapter Seven

The early days of Penelope's engagement passed like a golden dream.

Augusta was ecstatic! She had vowed to fire Miss Stride should the Earl ever propose to Penelope. But now that that glorious day had arrived, she felt strangely reluctant to do so. It was almost as if Augusta, having very little conscience, felt it necessary to hire a social one. Also she was shrewd enough to note that when she followed Miss Stride's strictures on decorum, society found her at least tolerable. There must be no more talk of hellfire, Miss Stride had told Augusta firmly. It was as well for Augusta that Mr. Manton was a gentleman and a friend of the Earl or she would be the laughingstock of London.

So Augusta had treated the surprised Penelope with a gentleness and kindness foreign to her cold and grasping nature, and Penelope returned this false warmth with all the gratitude of a very innocent heart.

The love match was the talk of the town. The Earl looked like a much younger man, the austere lines of his face softened with happiness. His young brother had given his blessing in no uncertain terms and the Earl did not know of Charles's relief. Augusta could have no more hold over the Viscount now that he had fulfilled his part of the bargain.

Augusta planned a lavish wedding. She also planned to move into the Earl's household as soon as he and Penelope were married, but she kept that part of the plan to herself.

One morning when Penelope was out driving with the Earl, Augusta received a caller in the shape of the Comte de Chernier. She clucked with irritation because Mr. Liwoski was just coming to the crucial part of the portrait.

She reluctantly ushered the Comte into a small study at the back of the house and then looked at him with shrewd hard eyes. The two blackmailers surveyed each other in silence for some minutes. The Comte was the first to speak.

"We have not been formally introduced," he said. "But I know you have heard of me. I also know you were hiding behind the screen that night at the Courtlands' ball.

"So Charles has done his part," he continued. "And your niece is to be a Countess. You, I gather, think you can hang onto her petticoats and climb the social ladder." He shook back the lace at his wrist and took a delicate pinch of snuff. "But that will not be the case, madam. Oh, dear me, no."

"What d'ye mean?" grated Augusta.

"It is like this, Madame Harvey . . . I may be seated? Yes?" He sat down on a high-backed chair and studied Augusta insolently. "The young couple is very much in love and very much *du monde.*"

"Speak English," snapped Augusta.

"Ah, well," he sighed. "Tell me, has the so elegant and grand Earl shown any sign that he would wish your company after he is married?"

"Course he will," said Augusta stoutly but experienced her first twinge of doubt. The Earl did indeed usually look at her as if she were something that had crept out of the back recesses of the kitchen stove.

"So little Charles has gone bleating to you," said Augusta nastily, deciding to attack. "Well, you traitor, I shall report you."

"You are a traitor yourself, if only by proxy," he sneered. "If I thought for a minute you would betray me, I would shoot you dead." He produced a long and lethal pistol and tossed it carelessly up and down in his long fingers.

"Pah!" said Augusta. "That toy don't frighten me. If you shoot me, you'd have to shoot all my servants as well. They know you're here."

"What is to stop me shooting you and leaving the country?" asked the Comte.

" 'Cause if your dirty work was finished, you'd have left long ago," replied Augusta. "You're wasting my time. Why did you really come here?"

"Because I do not like to see such a clever woman work so hard to achieve social recognition — and then fail."

"I'll *not* fail," said Augusta with grim echoes of Lady Macbeth.

"Oh, but you will, madam. The high and mighty Earl will drop you like a hot carriage brick as soon as his beloved Penelope is out from under your roof."

"So?" said Augusta with a fake yawn.

"So, my dear lady, the only answer is for you to enter the ranks of the aristocracy yourself."

"And how do I do that? Marry you?" sneered Augusta.

The Comte raised his hands, one of them still holding the pistol, in mock horror. "Heaven forbid!" he exclaimed. "But how would you like to be a Countess yourself?"

"Me! How?"

"You use your talents for snooping to good effect. The Earl has a great deal of high-ranking friends in the military. You supply me with little secrets, I supply them to the Bonapartistes and our very grateful Emperor will award you with a title and estates in France."

Augusta's eyes gleamed with a green light like a cat's. Then she shrugged her fat shoulders, wafting a smell of stale patchouli and sweat towards the Comte who wrinkled his long nose fastidiously. "Bonaparte's on Elba. He'll never get off. I'd need more proof than your word."

"Travel to France with me, tomorrow," said the Comte, leaning forward in his chair, "and you shall have that proof. You shall even see the estate that will be yours!"

"What'll I do with Penelope in the meantime? Not that I've said I'll go," said Augusta hurriedly.

"That's easy. Tell the enamored Earl to take the girl to see his country home. She will have to learn to supervise a great mansion after all. Then you will be free."

"I'm going to the Hart's ball with Penelope tonight," said Augusta. "Meet me there and I'll let you know my decision."

"As you wish," shrugged the Comte. "But I think you have already made up your mind!"

Augusta rang the bell and instructed the butler to show the Comte out and then returned to the drawing room where Mr. Liwoski was waiting impatiently.

The artist peered round his easel as Augusta seated herself and received a faint shock. Before, when Augusta had posed for him, she had primped her mouth into a small fashionable "o" and her eyes had been empty of expression. Now her mouth was stretched to its widest in an evil grin like a rictus, and her green eyes gleamed with a mixture of malice and power.

Mr. Liwoski shrugged. Miss Harvey wanted the picture completed that day and he had only time to paint what he saw. He rubbed on the canvas with his rag and then began to lay delicate brushstrokes, placing them as intricately and delicately patterned as a mosaic, and under his expert fingers he caught Augusta in all her glory.

Lady Hart tapped the Earl of Hestleton on the arm with her long fan. "Now, I could swear I did not invite that protégé of the Courtlands to my ball."

The Earl looked across the room and

spied the Comte de Chernier bowing to various acquaintances. "Then throw him out," he said laconically, turning his eyes away from the Comte to scan the room for Penelope.

"I do not wish to make a scene, Roger," said Lady Hart. "Perhaps you might . . ." She broke off with a sigh. For the Earl's face had become transfigured. Penelope Vesey had just walked into the room. She was wearing a rose pink silk gown, high-waisted in the current mode, with a spangled overdress floating around her slim figure in the evening breeze which drifted in through the long French windows opening onto the garden.

The Earl had forgotten about Lady Hart and the Comte, and indeed everyone else in the long ballroom. He had eyes only for Penelope. He crossed quickly to her side, and her face, turned up to his, glowed with love.

Penelope smiled up at him shyly, wondering for the hundredth time what this magnificent aristocrat could see in her. His black and white evening dress was faultless, from his intricate cravat to the sparkling jewels on his pumps. His copper hair seemed burnished till it burned with fiery lights and his gray eyes under their hooded lids held a message that made her pulses beat.

"A moment of your time, Roger," grated a voice in his ear.

Augusta Harvey stood smiling up at him. A faint look of hauteur at Miss Harvey's familiar use of his Christian name crossed his features. "What is it, Miss Harvey?" he demanded, none too graciously.

"I am thinking of taking a little holiday in France," said Augusta. "I've always wanted to see Paris and the countryside but I don't want to leave my little Penelope alone in Brook Street. Mayhap you could take her to your country home so that she'll get used to the running of a big house, like."

"Yes," said the Earl slowly. "As a matter of fact I have some unfinished business to attend to in the country. My maiden aunt, Matilda Jefferson, lives with me at the moment and would act as chaperone. When did you plan to leave, Miss Harvey?"

"Well, I'm having a party for the unveiling of my portrait," simpered Augusta. "Just a little informal affair with a few friends. I'm holding it in a couple of days' time. Let me see, that will be Saturday. And after that, I can leave. Say first thing on Sunday morning."

"Very well," said the Earl. "Does that

please you, my darling?"

"Oh, yes," smiled Augusta before Penelope could answer. Augusta thought the Earl had addressed the endearment to herself.

Augusta walked away, well satisfied, and Penelope collapsed into helpless giggles.

"I cannot wait to see Mr. Liwoski's portrait of Miss Harvey," said the Earl. "Now, my sweet, this next dance is a highly energetic Scottish reel. On the other hand, we could walk in the garden and do something ... er ... less energetic."

The Comte watched the Earl's well-tailored back disappearing through the French windows and waylaid Augusta Harvey.

"Roger is becoming quite fond of me," simpered Augusta. "He called me 'my darling.' "

"I am sure he was referring to his fiancée," said the Comte cooly, and watched with satisfaction as a little cloud of doubt settled on Augusta's brow. "Do not delude yourself, madam," he pursued. "The Earl will not have you in his household." He lowered his voice. "And if you travel with me, then I can show you the grand château that will be yours. Napoleon is generous to his friends. Think of it. No longer Miss Harvey but ...

Madame la Comtesse."

Augusta wavered. At that moment Lady Courtland sailed into view. Augusta dropped her a deep curtsey. Lady Courtland replied with a frozen stare and then raised her handkerchief pointedly to her nose before she stalked away. Augusta could not ignore this direct cut and her face flamed.

"I'll go," she said, glaring after Lady Courtland. "But not till Sunday, mind. My portrait is being exhibited on Saturday. You'll come, of course."

"Of course," said the Comte smoothly. "I sincerely hope the artist had done justice to your striking features."

From another corner of the ballroom Charles watched them and nervously bit his nails. He did not trust that combination of blackmailers one bit. His heart felt heavy and his head reeled from too much wine. He felt as if his world, never very secure, was falling apart. Every second, he dreaded the shout "spy!" As he tossed and turned at night, he saw the contempt that would be on the faces of his friends and the look of distaste and scorn on his brother's.

Yet he could not keep away from the gambling tables. He could not! He had already lost all the money he had won at Watier's and was in desperate need of more to satisfy his craving for the gaming table. Roger gave him a generous allowance but it was a pittance when one was playing against men who were prepared to gamble thousands in a night.

Then a little ray of hope crept into his mind. He had at least satisfied Augusta. Her niece was marrying his brother after all! He would call on Augusta before her portrait party and beg her to help him get rid of the Comte. Augusta was wily. She would think of something.

Augusta was by no means pleased to hear that the Viscount was desirous of having a few words with her before her famous party. Her lady's maid had just placed an enormous turban on Augusta's sparse locks which made her look rather like a bloated sultan. Augusta dashed the haresfoot over her face, sprinkling powder on her pink and red striped dress as she did so. Miss Stride had not been consulted as to suitable wear for the party, and Augusta had given free rein to her penchant for violent colors.

To complement the pink and red stripes of her gown, Augusta had chosen to wear an orange turban, decorated with a large synthetic ruby. She could never see the reason for wasting money on real jewels when fake ones looked just as pretty. She picked up an emerald green fan and stood patiently while her maid draped a purple gauze stole over her massive shoulders. She would see Charles. He had probably only come to cringe and flatter as usual.

Charles blinked rapidly. What looked like a particularly violent sunset erupted into the room as Augusta entered in all her glory.

The ill-assorted pair stared at each other in silence. Where there is a bully, there is always someone who seems to crave to be bullied; whose shrinking soul and very emanations seem to cry out to the bully for a harder hit. Such was Charles, Viscount Clairmont. And Augusta reacted to this quivering psyche as all bullies will react. Her eyes gleamed with a lazy enjoyment of power and the knowledge that there was one person at least who must suffer the worst of her manners without complaint.

"What d'ye want?" she said.

"What a splendid gown, Miss Harvey," babbled Charles. "I've never seen anything like it before. You have such a fine eye for color. You . . ."

"I asked you what you wanted," snarled Augusta.

"Oh, well, I mean, I hope you're pleased

that I've paid my part of the bargain. I mean, Penelope's to be married and all that."

"So?"

"Well, I mean, we're square, aren't we? After all, you won't tell Roger anything now?"

"Who says I won't," said Augusta with a slow grin splitting her powdered cheeks. "That was only your first task," went on this heartless female Eurystheus. "I've still got use for you. Now, the Comte wants me to get secrets for him. But I can't crawl around Horseguards and the Foreign Office the way you can, and why keep a dog and bark yourself, heh! So you'll do my work for me."

"No!" screamed Charles. "I can't bear it. *Don't make me!* I swear I'll take my life. Have you never heard of a conscience? At first it did not matter. Just one little bit of information, that was all. But now, I am a fully fledged traitor. Good God, woman! We are betraying England!"

"Oh, tol rol!" sneered Augusta. "Such heroics." She got to her feet and stood over Charles who was crouched on a low chair. She suddenly seemed immense and powerful. "You snivelling little coward," she said, "prating on about patriotism while you foul up my drawing room and shit your small clothes with fear. Harkee, laddie, you will do what I want and when I want it or Roger shall hear about you. He can't touch me because he would have to expose you and he's too proud of his great name to do that. Take yourself off. You *puking* little baby."

She began to laugh, a loud, horrible, jeering sound which rang and rang in Charles's ears as he crept from the room.

He reeled across the hall, unaware that Penelope was standing on the staircase staring at his distraught face in amazement, and out of the door into the street.

Penelope stood very still. What was wrong with Charles? And why was her aunt laughing in that terrible way?

She went into the drawing room. Augusta had stopped laughing and was adjusting her turban in front of the looking glass. Penelope winced at the violent color combination and then said, "Tell me, dear Aunt, is there anything the matter with Charles? I saw him leaving just now and he looked so very white."

"No," said Augusta. "He is in fine fettle and delighted with your engagement, my dear — as are we all." She came towards the girl and put a plump arm around Penelope's slender waist and gave her a playful squeeze.

"I'll be sorry to lose my little niece but, after all, Auntie will be staying with you for long, long visits. *Won't she?*"

"Oh — oh, yes, that is — well, Roger says we should be on our own — together that is — for . . . for some time so that we can get to know each other," said Penelope, looking at the floor. The Earl had, in fact, warned Penelope that, despite her improved manners, he could only stand a very, very little of Augusta's presence.

Augusta took note of Penelope's downcast eyes and the hesitancy with which she had spoken and became more than ever resolved to depart for France in the morning.

One by one the guests began to arrive until the drawing room was quite crowded. Miss Stride was there, and the Earl. Other members of the *ton* had accepted Miss Harvey's invitation out of curiosity and because the Earl was one of the highest members of society. Eyes kept turning to the draped easel at the end of the room. Only the artist had failed to put in an appearance.

The door opened and everyone turned. But it was only Charles, his face still very white. The Earl looked at his brother anxiously and then gave a mental shrug. Charles spent such late nights drinking with his cronies that he often looked white and shaken the next day.

At last Augusta could wait no longer. Mr. Liwoski had obviously decided not to attend, which was strange since he had not been paid and had not let Augusta see the portrait, having promised her a glorious surprise on the day of the unveiling.

Augusta gave a loud cough to collect everyone's attention. "My lord, ladies and gentlemen," she said in a voice quite squeaky with excitement. "I shall perform the unveiling of the portrait myself."

She grasped the edge of the cloth which covered the easel and pulled.

There was sudden silence.

Penelope stood rooted to the floor, gazing in horror at the portrait.

The paint had been laid on by the hand of a genius. The figure in the portrait seemed alive. The painted Augusta Harvey stared at the room full of guests, her face a mask of hatred, cunning, and malice.

The real Augusta Harvey looked proudly up at her painted self, seeing nothing amiss. It was, after all, a face that often stared back at her from her looking glass.

Then the silence was hideously shattered. Charles let out a high, thin, screaming, spluttering laugh. With a shaking finger he pointed to the canvas.

"Augusta Harvey to the life," he screamed. "By God, Augusta, the man has painted your soul!"

The Earl hurried towards his brother and then, taking his arm in a firm grip, led him from the room.

The guests all burst out into noisy speech.

Penelope stood quite still, staring at the portrait. Her own feelings for Augusta had swung back and forth as her still undeveloped personality swung from maturity to immaturity — one minute the woman, the next the child. The woman felt that Augusta should be watched very carefully and not trusted very much. The child longed for Augusta to be a substitute mother and saw in her coarseness a rough diamond. Which was the real Augusta?

Penelope did not know.

But as she continued to stare at the portrait, she began to feel afraid.

Chapter Eight

Wyndham Court, home of the Earl of Hestleton, was a great rambling pile of mixed architecture, from Tudor to modern. It stood on a rise, commanding a fine view of the fields and woods of Hertfordshire.

Here was the home Penelope had dreamed of, with its long, spacious rooms and bowls of flowers.

She had at first been intimidated by the army of servants and the rather grim and austere figure of Aunt Matilda who was an extremely tall, thin elderly spinster. But the servants had done all in their power to make the future mistress of Wyndham Court feel at home and Aunt Matilda had turned out to be garrulous and friendly and not at all like her forbidding exterior.

The weather was idyllic, long hot sunny days fading into soft gray and rose evenings and starlit nights.

Penelope had spent her days being driven around the estate by the Earl and her evenings playing the piano for Aunt Matilda who had an insatiable love of music. And then, sometimes, in a quiet corner of the garden there were those stolen, hungry kisses with the Earl. Each time they seemed not enough, and Penelope would toss and turn during the night, feeling strangely restless and unsatisfied.

It was not that Aunt Matilda was a particularly conscientious chaperone. It was just that she had taken a great liking to Penelope, trotting happily after her when Penelope retired for the night and passing half an hour each night in Penelope's bedroom "having a comfortable coze."

Early one evening Penelope escaped from Aunt Matilda's company and went out onto the broad flagged terrace to enjoy the cool, still air. Scarlet roses spilled over the edge of great stone urns on the balustrade of the terrace, and beyond, the wide, green, shaven lawns rolled gently away towards the darkness of the woods.

Penelope heard a step on the terrace behind her and a well-loved voice said, "Dreaming, my dear?"

Penelope turned, her pale skin almost translucent in the soft twilight. "Oh, Roger," she sighed. "Of all things to think about on this beautiful evening! But I can't help wondering why Mr. Liwoski painted Aunt Augusta *so*. He did not seem a particularly malicious man. He made her look *evil*."

"It was a caricature, that was all," said the Earl mildly.

"But it could not be that," expostulated Penelope. "A caricature dramatises, *highlights,* qualities that are *there*. And Aunt is not malicious or evil."

Her voice rose at the end in a faint question. "There is no accounting for the whims of artists," said the Earl lightly.

At that moment they heard Aunt Matilda calling them in to dinner. While she regaled Penelope with a recipe for rose water, the Earl sat buried in thought, remembering the aftermath of the portrait party.

Augusta's portrait! Charles had been nearly incoherent. "But don't you see, Roger? Don't you see the joke of it all," he had kept saying over and over again. "It's the pig lady in person."

The pig-faced lady was one of the absurd reports and ridiculous stories which had swept London during the spring of 1814. Everyone knew someone who knew someone who had seen the pig-faced lady. The shops were full of caricatures of her wearing a poke bonnet with a large veil, with "A pig in a poke" written underneath. A timid young baronet, Sir William Elliot, claimed that the pig-faced lady lived in Grosvenor Square. He had met her when he had called at a certain mansion and had been unable to restrain his cry of horror when what he thought was a fashionably dressed young person turned to reveal the monstrous and horrible face of a pig. He claimed that the pig-faced lady, incensed at his cry of horror, had rushed towards him with great grunts and had bitten him in the neck. The wound had been dressed by Hawkins, the surgeon, in St. Audley Street and Mr. Hawkins had said the wound was a severe one.

Sir William, however, claimed to have forgotten the exact address in Grosvenor Square.

For days after, several bucks and bloods had hung around the confines of Grosvenor Square hoping for a glance at this lady, but in vain. The story spread all over London. The pig-faced lady had been seen at the Tower, at Gunter's eating ices, even at Almack's!

The Earl realised that if Charles continued in this hysterical vein, most of London would be flooding to Brook Street for a glimpse of Augusta Harvey.

He finally seemed to have driven some

sense into Charles's head, and when his young brother appeared calmer, had asked him the meaning of the outburst. Charles had looked slightly furtive and had claimed that he had been foxed and the Earl remembered that his brother *had* smelled of brandy.

The Earl turned his thoughts to the more pleasant prospect of the present. He looked down the long table to where Penelope sat at the other end and could not help comparing her with her aunt. The girl radiated innocence and sweetness. Her manners were well-bred and refined and her voice, soft and gentle.

He considered himself very lucky indeed as he watched the soft candlelight playing on her delicate features, and he forgot all his worries about Charles and Augusta. London seemed very far away with its noise and bustle and dirt.

"My dear, *do* try this buttered crab," Aunt Matilda was saying as she helped herself to another plateful. Penelope shook her head. Aunt Matilda seemed to be able to eat a vast amount of food for such a thin lady.

"As I was saying," Aunt Matilda droned on, "it is most necessary to call on sick tenants *in person*. Of course one can go too far. Now, Lady Barbara Desmond over at

Suthers carried it to extremes and *would* go even if they had the smallpox and, of course, she died. Not of smallpox, dear, cholera it was. An excess of zeal. *An excess of zeal!* Do have some more buttered crab. Oh, I have already asked you that. Then I had better finish it myself. It is *too rich* for the servants, you know, and might give them ideas above their station. And it is *very bad* for people to get ideas above their station. I trust, my dear, you would have escaped the contagion emanating from Godwin, Wollstonecraft, Holcroft, Thelwell, and the writers of that *pestilential* school. But then the servants do not read much — if they can read *at all* — and, believe me, buttered crab is famous for arousing radical notions in the palates of those unaccustomed to it!"

"Really," teased Penelope, "it is the first time I have heard of anyone's palate having radical notions."

"But it sends *the message to the brain*," said Aunt Matilda earnestly. "It says 'Arise! Lead the *aristos* to the *lanterne,* bring out *la guillotine,* you too can dine on buttered crab!' You *do* understand now, don't you?"

"Yes," said Penelope faintly. A choked sound came from the Earl.

"Of course, there are other messages from food. Quite pleasant ones," went on Aunt

Matilda. "I was once in love, my dear. Hard to believe, when you look at me now," she added sadly, tucking a wisp of gray hair under her lace cap. "But I was. Yes, indeed. And with the curate, too. Most unsuitable and of course Papa was *quite right* although naturally I did not think so at the time. When he came to tea, Mama always served macaroon cakes. Macaroon cakes and tea. Now every time I taste a macaroon, I still feel very young and lost and sort of trembly, you know." Aunt Matilda fell silent as she stared back down the years.

Penelope looked down the table and found her gaze held by the Earl. She began to feel very young and lost and trembly as well. How long could the Earl, who was used to experienced liaisons with experienced women, be content with mere kisses? How long could she?

Penelope sighed and became aware that Aunt Matilda had roused herself from her reverie.

"What a monstrous amount of food I have consumed," said that lady. "Now, shall we go into the drawing room, Penelope, and leave Roger to his port. And you shall play something for me."

The Earl rose as well and grasped the decanter. "You are not having Penelope's beautiful music all to yourself tonight, Aunt," he said. "I shall join you."

Soon the rippling notes of Vivaldi echoed round the drawing room, and the Earl stretched out his long legs and admired his fiancée and wished they could be married by special license that very night.

Suddenly a loud snore interrupted the music and Penelope stopped and swung round. Aunt Matilda had fallen fast asleep, her cap tipped over one eye and her mouth open.

The Earl moved slowly towards Penelope, his face lit with a mischievous smile. "Our chaperone has gone to sleep," he whispered, "and I have been longing to kiss you all day."

He drew Penelope to her feet and wrapped his arms around her and kissed her long and hard until they were both dizzy. "I can't stand much more of this frustration," muttered the Earl finally with his mouth against hers. "I. . . ."

"*Roger!*" Aunt Matilda was awake, her face suffused with a delicate pink. "You are to be married quite soon, dear boy, so you should curb your . . . well, till . . . well never mind. 'Tis not genteel to talk of such things in company. Come, Penelope, I shall see you to your bedchamber and we shall have a comfortable coze.

"In fact, I think we should *go now*. It must have been the duckling!" she said triumphantly, pausing in the doorway. "Duckling is inflammatory! Very. Good night, Roger. Come, my dear, what was I saying. Dear me, I do forget things these days. A sad sign of getting old. Oh, yes, chaperone, Roger. Watch that step, my dear, it wobbles so and I have told the servants to fix it and they say they have, but there, it wobbles just the same and one could so easily get a turned ankle.

"As I was saying, has your aunt discussed the Delicate Side of Marriage with you? No? Then . . . ah here we are." She sat down heavily on a chair. "Put my candle on the mantelpiece, my dear. Don't ring for the maid yet. I must tell you, you see. There are certain things that are Right after marriage and Wrong before marriage. Now, 'twas most embarrassing for the Wiltons over at Hadley Hall when Sally was married to young Brothers and her wedding gown stuck out in front in *such* a fashion. Of course, they claimed she was wearing a *pad* but no one has worn them since I was a girl when it was fashionable to look six months pregnant. And she *was!* So there. I am glad we have had this little coze. You see, someone has to tell you, and I am so very fond of you."

Penelope, who had been opening and shutting her mouth, trying to get a word in edgeways during this rather incoherent lecture, gave it up as a bad job and kissed Aunt Matilda's withered cheek before that lady sailed from the room with a smug smile on her face, indicating that she felt she had just completed a distasteful task and had done it well.

But after the maid had prepared her for bed, Penelope stood for a long time, looking out of the window into the garden and leaning her hot forehead against the cool glass. Her body seemed to be trembling with unrealised, unknown, and unfulfilled passion. Too much kissing, she thought. Too much sudden restraint on the Earl's part. Too much of suddenly putting her away from him. They were soon to be married after all. Why was it then considered a sin to do more than kiss? Perhaps she, Penelope, was not a lady after all!

A glimmer of white in the garden below caught her eye. Her room was on the second floor and had a little wrought-iron balcony with long windows in the French manner. She pulled a wrap round her shoulders and drew open the windows. The iron of the balcony felt cold on her bare feet and a cool breeze sent her long nightdress billowing about her legs.

The Earl of Hestleton was walking backwards and forwards below her window. He was wearing a cambric shirt, open at the throat, leather breeches, and top boots.

A ripple of laughter escaped Penelope, and he quickly looked up. "You look like a pirate," she said in a soft whisper which carried to his ears on the still night air.

He stood with his hands on his hips, looking up at her, his head thrown back. He did not say anything, only stood there, looking up at her very intently, his gray eyes gleaming silver in the bright moonlight.

Penelope stared back at him, her heart beginning to thud against her ribs. She knew what the look meant and the unspoken question in his eyes.

She gave a funny jerky little nod of her head and he moved deliberately forward and seized the creeper which grew against the wall and began to climb.

Penelope retreated to her room and sat very solemnly on the edge of the bed.

He climbed in at the window and then stood in front of her, looking down.

She rose to her feet and threw herself into his arms, her body trembling down the length of him. "Faith, I no longer know myself," she whispered. "I love you, Roger."

He lifted her gently in his arms and laid

her on the bed and then lay down beside her, stroking her shaking body and muttering husky endearments and then kissing her and kissing her till the world went away.

At last he tried to move away, but she cling onto him desperately, her arms wound round his neck.

"Oh, dear heart," said the Earl, "how on earth am I going to make love to you with all my clothes on?"

Penelope drew away from him and said with a shaky laugh, "It must have been the duckling."

And, "Three cheers for the duckling!" said the Earl of Hestleton as his shirt and breeches followed his top boots onto the floor.

The stay at Wyndham Court was over and the Earl and Penelope drove slowly back into summer London in an ecstatic silence. Everything looked crystal clear and new, fresh minted in the sunlight.

Augusta Harvey had returned from France and the Earl did not want his perfect happiness to be marred by a social visit to Miss Harvey. He kissed Penelope's hand as he left her on her doorstep and reminded her again that he would be calling on her on the following day to take her to the peace celebrations in Hyde Park.

He then drove to Grosvenor Square and whistling a jaunty tune, strode into his mansion.

"My lord," said his butler who had let him into the hall, "I am very worried about Lord Charles."

"Why, what's he been up to now?" asked the Earl, stripping off his York tan gloves and handing his bat and cane to the butler.

"Lord Charles has been in the study, my lord. There was a strange report from the room and I tried the door, but it was locked."

"He's probably in his cups and falling over the furniture or writing love letters to some *inamorato*," said the Earl cheerfully. He walked across the hall and rattled the study door, calling out, "Charles! Hey, Charles! It's me, little brother. Let me in!"

Silence.

"Charles!" he cried again in a voice suddenly sharpened with anxiety.

The house suddenly seemed very still and quiet.

The Earl drew back and crashed his booted foot against the panels of the door and kicked, kicked again, until the door splintered and flew open.

What was left of Charles, Viscount

Clairmont's head was lying buried in his arms. He was slumped across a pretty little escritoire.

A broad shaft of sunlight lit up the scene with an unreal clarity. The room was absolutely quiet except for the steady drip, drip, drip of blood onto the floor.

Charles had thrown his last dice and turned his last card. But in all his wasted life of idleness and failure, he had at last made a thorough job of just one thing. With an unerring aim and steady hand, he had blown his brains out.

Chapter Nine

The regent had ordered great peace celebrations in Hyde Park, St. James's Park, and Green Park which were decorated with Oriental temples, towers, pagodas, and bridges. There were balloon ascents, a miniature naval battle on the Serpentine, and a hundred-foot-high Castle of Discord "with all its horrors of fire and destruction" which finally thinned out in smoke to reveal a Temple of Concord.

Penelope saw nothing of this except great bursts of fireworks which sent their thousands of stars cascading over London and lit up her white face as she sat in the corner of the window seat. The Earl had not come. And since the servants had been allowed the day off to watch the celebrations, she had no one to send to ask the Earl what had happened.

At last she could bear it no longer. Wrapped in a long cloak, she slipped from the house and made her way through the deserted streets to Grosvenor Square. All the world and his wife seemed to have taken to the parks.

Penelope's first awareness that something was badly wrong was when she approached the Earl's great mansion and found that the pavement and the road had been thickly strewn with straw to muffle the wheels of the passing carriages.

Someone must be ill! Surely not the Earl.

Then with a lurch at her heart she saw that a grim lozenge-shaped board had been hammered up over the drawing room window.

A hatchment!

Death!

Standing still, with her feet in the straw, Penelope stared up at the board, trying to make out the coat of arms on the hatchment. Then she slowly dragged her way up the steps and rapped on the knocker.

Rourke, the Earl's butler, answered the door, and Penelope's frightened eyes flew to the black band on his arm.

"Roger," she whispered. "What has happened to Roger?"

"It is not my master," said Rourke coldly, his usually pleasant face like a mask. "My young lord, the Viscount Clairmont, is dead, Miss Vesey."

"What happened?" asked Penelope, trying to suppress a guilty feeling of relief.

"A seizure of the heart, miss," said Rourke. "And now if you will excuse me . . ."

"But Roger . . . where is Roger?" cried Penelope. "I must go to him."

She made to cross the hall, but Rourke barred her way.

"I am very sorry, miss," he said, "but I have instructions from the Earl that you are not to be admitted."

Penelope stared at him, wide-eyed, and then raised a trembling hand to her mouth. "Roger? Not see me?" she said faintly. "You must be mistaken."

"No, miss," replied the butler with an impassive face. "My instructions are very clear."

He politely held the street door wide open and inclined his head.

He then stood on the doorstep and watched as the slight figure of Penelope was swallowed up in the darkness of the empty square.

"Rourke!" The butler turned at the sound of his master's voice and, shutting the street door, walked towards the drawing room.

The Earl sat slumped in a George Smith armchair in front of the fire, his long fingers grasping the brass sphinxes on the armrests so tightly that his knuckles showed white.

"That was Miss Vesey," he said in a flat voice.

"What did she want?"

The butler cleared his throat. "Miss Vesey did not know of the death of Lord Charles, my lord. When I told her — as . . . er . . . per instructions — that my young lord had been taken of a seizure, she asked to see you, my lord. I informed her of your lordship's instructions, and Miss Vesey left."

"Who was with her?" demanded the Earl harshly. "That great, fat, white spider, Augusta Harvey?"

"No, my lord. Miss Vesey was not even accompanied by a maid."

The Earl stared for some moments into the empty fireplace and, as Rourke was about to retire, he turned in his chair and faced the butler squarely. Rourke was taken aback by the bitterness in his set, white face. "I trust you *have* obeyed my instructions," said the Earl. "Only you and I, the undertaker and the doctor, Rourke, know of how Charles took his life — and only you and I know of the letter he left. I would not like you to forget . . ."

"Indeed, my lord," said Rourke, "I am in no danger of *ever* forgetting."

And indeed the butler thought that scene would be burned into his brain until the day he died. He could still see the shattered mess that had been Lord Charles slumped over the desk, and the Earl standing over him, reading a letter. The Earl had looked up as Rourke had entered the room and had silently handed him the letter. Rourke had been in his father's employ and had known the Earl since he was a baby.

The handwriting had been very shaky but the reason Charles had taken his own life had been all too clear. "My dear Roger," he had written. "I have been working as a Bonapartiste spy. Augusta Harvey found out, but said she would not tell anyone, provided I made sure you married her niece, Penelope. Augusta and Penelope planned to enter the social world via a good marriage. But Augusta will never let me go. This is the only way I can escape her and escape bringing disgrace on our name. Forgive me, Roger." Here the writing had trailed away in a pathetic line of blots.

In a cold, metallic voice the Earl had rapped out his instructions. The manner of Charles's death must be kept a secret — and Penelope Vesey must never again be allowed to cross the threshold. Rourke had been appalled at the idea of Augusta getting off

Scot-free, but the Earl had pointed out that to drag Augusta through the courts would only bring shame on Charles's memory. "I am sure Charles did not pass on any information worth anything," he had said. "He was always dropping in on Horseguards to visit old Witherspoon and Witherspoon knows no secrets at all but is excellent at making them up while he is in his cups."

The Earl however had vowed to call on a certain Comte de Chernier, only to find that the Comte had mysteriously disappeared.

Now he wearily turned over in his mind the final arrangements for Charles's funeral. The doctor, long in service to the family, had been persuaded to give a certificate of death from natural causes. The Earl would convey Charles's body to Wyndham Court in the morning where it would be placed in the family vault. But before he departed, he had a letter to write, a letter that should shatter the social-climbing ambitions of Miss Harvey and her niece.

Rourke quietly left the room, softly closing the double doors while the Earl sat like a statue, remembering Penelope's laughter and the feel of her young body in his arms. He realised with a shock that when she had sung that song, "The Harlot's Progress," on the first night they had met, she had not been trying to antagonise him but merely revealing herself in her true colors. She has the body of a virgin but the soul of a harlot, he thought savagely. The very thought of her filled him with complete and utter disgust.

He moved wearily over to a kneehole Chippendale writing table at the window and began to sharpen a quill. "My *dear* Penelope," he began . . .

Penelope put down the letter the following day with trembling fingers and then picked it up again, although she already knew each bitter and acid word by heart.

"My *dear* Penelope," she read. "Although I enjoyed our pastoral idyll, I feel, on reflection, that we should not suit. Our social backgrounds are too far apart and, although I much enjoyed your favors, my dear, I would much prefer a lady as my Countess. Please send a notice of the termination of our engagement to the *Gazette.* I am sure it would be too embarrassing for both of us should we meet again. To that end, I have told my butler to refuse you admittance. You will realise I have your best wishes at heart. I remain Yr. Most

Humble and Devoted Servant, Roger, Earl of Hestleton."

Augusta bustled into the room and looked sharply at Penelope's white face and then at the letter in her hands.

"What is it?" she demanded.

Penelope silently handed her the letter. Augusta read it closely and then gave a harsh laugh. "Pay no attention. His brother is dead, did you know?"

Penelope nodded.

"Well then. He's feeling bitter, that's all. He'll come around. There's something havey-cavey about young Charles's death, though. My footman had it from Hestleton's footman that there was the sound of a shot from the study and nobody's been allowed to see the body." Her protruding eyes narrowed as she looked at the letter again.

"He says here he enjoyed your favors. What favors?" she rapped.

Penelope dropped her eyes. She would never, ever tell anyone what had really happened or her life would indeed be ruined — if it could possibly be ruined more than it was already.

"As an engaged couple," she whispered, "we naturally were very affectionate."

"How affectionate?" demanded Augusta, coming to stand over her trembling niece.

"A few kisses, that is all," whispered Penelope.

"You *fool*," sneered Augusta. "You should have got him into bed and kept him there. Well, we must play his little game. I'll send a notice, cancelling the engagement. But, harkee, I'm not going to waste all the blunt I laid out on a wardrobe for you, miss. I thought to send you packing if ever you failed to nab the Earl. But I'm not doing so badly on my own with Euphemia Stride to monitor me. Though why a body isn't allowed to open her own mouth, I can't say. Euphie says if I just sit still and say nothing, 'tis better. So, now we come to you.

"I had hoped, you see, that you would marry the Earl and, who knows, you may yet. In fact, that was why I asked you to London. I would then have used the Earl to get invited to all the best houses."

She rattled on, unaware of Penelope's stricken face. "Don't worry. I ain't going to send you packing . . . *yet*. It so happens that Lord Barrington was saying to Miss Stride only the other day that you was 'a demned fine-looking gel' and it occurs to me, we might go further and fare worse than to have my Lord Barrington as your beau."

"But Lord Barrington is married, he's about sixty, and he has a terrible reputation as a roué," gasped Penelope.

"His wife is ailing," said Augusta cynically, "and Barrington is invited everywhere."

Penelope shook her head in bewilderment. She could not quite believe her eyes as she stared at her aunt. It was as if the painted Augusta had stepped down from her picture frame.

"Let me see if I understand you, Aunt," said Penelope slowly. "For some reason, you do not seem to find Roger's rejection of me strange . . ."

"Get it into your head that the engagement's at an end," said Augusta brutally. "That kind of aristocrat don't like common blood being injected into their families, God rot 'em. But as I said, he may come round yet, but I don't aim to put any money on it. You've still got a roof over your head and clothes on your back so what more's bothering you?"

"I thought you cared for me," said Penelope in a low voice. "Now you tell me that you are simply using me to further your social ambitions and want me to consort with an elderly, married roué."

"You don't mince your words, do you?"

smiled Augusta. "So I'll let you have it in plain language. I only care for what your pretty face can get us in the way of a title. I would tell you not to cancel the engagement and sue the Earl for breach of promise but that will get us nowhere. Not with that high and mighty Lord's connections. And while we're waiting around to see what he'll do, Lord Barrington may escape. Be reasonable. You don't have to work for a living and there's plenty more fish in the sea. I'll have you married yet. If you don't like it, you can get out!"

Penelope thought desperately, fighting against the waves of shock that engulfed her; first the Earl's letter, now this. But she was sure Roger had made a mistake about her, had heard some malicious gossip. He could not have murmured all those words of love or have made all those plans for their future life together unless he were sincere. Made cunning by desperation, and determined to stay in London until she could at least see Roger again, Penelope schooled her face as she raised her eyes to her aunt.

"I will do what you say, Aunt," she said in a trembling voice. "Only, do not expect me to see Lord Barrington immediately. I am very upset over Roger."

"You'll get over it," said Augusta cynically. "And who knows, I may be a Countess before you."

Penelope stared at her aunt in amazement. "Are you considering marrying, Aunt?"

Augusta bit her fat lip. How easy it was to let secrets slip. But she could not resist saying, "Just you wait and see, my girl. Just you wait and see."

Penelope picked up the letter and her sewing and left the room. She could not stand to be in her aunt's presence a minute longer. She had forgiven Augusta her many vulgarities and rudenesses, believing that Augusta was underneath kind and generous and had only the welfare of her niece at heart. Had she not been so determined to meet the Earl again, face-to-face, Penelope would have left the house that minute.

Augusta watched the girl as she left the room and noticed Penelope's white face and the droop of her shoulders.

I hope she doesn't mope too long, thought Augusta. She'll spoil all those marketable good looks if she goes on pining.

She turned her mind to the mystery of Charles's death. The Comte de Chernier had left London as soon as he had heard the news and had gone into hiding in a villa in Barnet where he was known as Mr. Cobbett.

144

He had told Augusta that he did not for one minute believe Charles had had a seizure, but that he had probably taken his own life and left a note. Why, Charles had been threatening just such a thing the day before his death! "The Earl can't do much to you," the Comte had said to her, "but I wouldn't put it past the Earl to come looking for me with a brace of pistols if Charles told him anything about me! Try to find out what you can about Charles's death."

Augusta reflected that it would be just like a snivelling weakling like Charles to commit suicide. He had certainly behaved like a madman at her portrait party. Augusta had found nothing amiss with her portrait and was very proud of it indeed, and a very surprised Mr. Liwoski had received his fee instead of the scene he expected. He had not meant to paint such a monster, but Augusta had not given him any time to lie with paintbrush and so he had portrayed simply what he had seen.

Augusta looked fondly up at her portrait above the fireplace as she waited for the return of her footman, Snyle. She had given Snyle a quantity of money and instructions to buy Rourke, the Earl's butler, as many drinks as possible and to find out the secret of Viscount Clairmont's death. Snyle had informed her that today was the butler's day off, the Earl having taken only his valet with him to the country and that although Rourke was as closemouthed as an oyster, he had a weakness for drink which he only indulged in his free time.

It was now late afternoon, and Snyle had been gone since midday.

At last Augusta saw the powdered head of her footman passing the drawing room window. In a few moments Snyle sidled into the room. He was a thin tall man with a pockmarked face and eyes as cunning as Augusta's own.

"I got what you wanted, mum," he said triumphantly.

"Out with it!" commanded Augusta.

Snyle had indeed been successful in lubricating the Earl's butler to the maudlin point where the butler had drunkenly muttered out the secret of Charles's death. Augusta listened with her eyes gleaming. It gave her a delicious feeling of power. But her enjoyment fled as her eyes met the malicious eyes of the servant.

"What are you staring at me like that for?" she snapped.

"There was a note, mum," said Snyle running a pale tongue over his lips. "Lord Charles said in it how he was a Bonapartiste spy and how you'd been blackmailing him to get the Earl to marry Miss Vesey."

"And so?" queried Augusta with sudden amiability, but thinking, So *that* is why the Earl terminated the engagement!

"And so, mum, to put it bluntly — it's going to cost you a packet to get me to keep my mouth shut."

Augusta slapped her knee and gave a jolly laugh. "If you ain't a one, Snyle," she said with great good humor, and, fumbling for something in her large reticule, she got to her feet. "Well, you're as bad as me, no doubt of that. We may as well have a drink to seal the bargain."

She picked up a decanter from the side table and stood with her back to him. "Not that I suppose you'll appreciate this. It's a good vintage."

She poured a glass and Snyle took it from her. This was all going easier than he had thought. His fortune was made. He took a great draft of wine, his eyes bulged hideously, and then his feet performed a mad dance on the floor. His back arched and his face turned purple. He clawed at his cravat and then fell lifeless to the floor.

Lucky I had that poison handy, said Augusta to herself. And to think that Euphie Stride gave it to me to put down rats!

She dragged the footman over to a corner behind a sofa and then, pulling a holland cover out of a cupboard, she threw it over the servant's body and then rang the bell.

When her butler appeared, she told that surprised man that she wanted the house to herself for the evening and that all the servants could go to Hyde Park again to see the peace celebrations which were still going on.

She then sat, after he had left, watching the pale light deepening to blue on the narrow street outside, listening for the sounds of the servants leaving by the area steps.

In the little music room across the hallway, Penelope was playing a jaunty song from Mozart's opera, *The Magic Flute*, but singing the words so sadly that she might as well have been playing a dirge.

A bustling, a rap of heels, and shouts of laughter moving up the area steps and then diminishing along the street told Augusta that all the servants had finally left. She got to her feet and moved quickly across the dark hallway to the music room. The key was in the door outside and Augusta softly turned it and locked the door.

Then she returned to the drawing room and, with surprising strength, hefted the body of Snyle up onto her back. She crossed the hallway with her macabre burden. The flickering light from the parish lamp in the street outside threw the shadow of Augusta with the servant on her back dancing up the stairs, like some great humpbacked monster. Augusta paused with her head on one side as Penelope began to sing again.

"Only friendship's harmony," Penelope sang sadly,

"Softens every sorrow.
We without this sympathy,
Ne'er could face tomorrow!"

"Pretty," thought Augusta, momentarily diverted. "Very pretty."

She made her way to the cellar door and kicked it open. She dropped her bundle at the top of the cellar stairs and went to fetch a branch of candles.

Still leaving the dead servant at the top of the stairs, Augusta went down into the cellar and looked around until she found what she wanted. She then climbed up the cellar stairs, collected the body, and lumbered back down with it. She dropped her burden again and pried open the top of a cask of canary. With a great heave she got the body of Snyle back on her shoulders and then slowly slid it into the barrel, moving quickly back as a wave of wine slopped over the side. Then she hammered the lid back down and marked the barrel with a red cross.

Augusta cared little for literature or books but she had to admit that sometimes Shakespeare came in handy. She had recently seen Edmund Kean in *Richard III* and had much enjoyed seeing "false, fleeting, perjur'd Clarence" ending up in the butt of malmsey.

She retreated up the stairs, locked the cellar door, unlocked the music room, and then sat down in the drawing room to wait.

From the music room Penelope's sad voice, raised in song, echoed plaintively through the dark house.

"Ah, I know it, all is gone now,
Gone forever love divine!
Now no more sweet hours of rapture
Come to cheer this heart of mine!"

I wonder how long she's going to mope, thought Augusta.

Then she heard the sounds she had been waiting for. The servants were returning home.

She waited a few minutes and rang the bell. When the butler answered her summons, she told him that there was a cask of canary in the cellar marked with a red cross.

150

"I want you to get two of the strongest footmen," said Augusta, "to take that particular cask out to Barnet in the morning. They are to deliver it to a Mr. Cobbett at the Willows with my compliments. The cask is made of a special wood so it is very heavy. Tell the men to be careful."

After all, reflected Augusta when the butler had left, a French spy should have more knowledge of how to dispose of a body than she herself!

Chapter Ten

The weary summer dragged on and still the Earl did not return to town.

Hyde Park was changed from a green oasis to a sort of crumbling dusty desert set about with temporary taverns. After the peace celebrations, every drinking place in town which had taken up temporary residence in the park had decided, it seemed, to make their stay permanent. Where green grass had grown, now were long rows of dirty, evil-smelling booths. The visits of foreign royalties went on, and people complained they could no longer get their clothes washed as all the washerwomen were working for Kings and Princes, and milk was in short supply because, it was said, the cows in Green Park were being frightened by the perpetual cheering and fireworks.

Augusta assiduously accepted every invitation she could get and by dint of only opening her mouth to make some quiet flattering comment, and by creeping around the houses of the great and searching in their bureaus, came up with a surprising amount of useful information for the Comte.

It came as a great surprise to Augusta, however, and a greater surprise to Miss Stride, when an invitation with an imposing crest arrived in Brook Street. Miss Harvey and Miss Vesey were invited to a party to be held by the Prince Regent at Clarence House.

Augusta's joy knew no bounds. She began to berate Penelope on that young lady's dismal looks. It was time Penelope came out of mourning for her lost engagement and performed her duties as Augusta's niece.

Both ladies were to be squired to Clarence House by Lord Barrington, and Penelope was warned to be very civil to that gentleman.

Penelope felt she was past caring about anything and when the great evening arrived, numbly accepted Lord Barrington's heavy gallantries. Lord Barrington was a tall, thin man with a painted face and powdered hair and eyes like a lizard. When he spoke in his high, mincing voice, he had a habit of curling his long tongue up to the roof of his mouth at the end of each sentence which added to his reptilian appearance.

Penelope was in court dress, black muslin over a rose silk underskirt. Lord Barrington had presented her with a diamond pendant which she wore at her throat, having no strength of will left to refuse his gift. She had written several pleading little letters to the Earl, but all had been returned to her, unopened.

The party was held in a special hall at Carlton House, built by Nash for the occasion. The walls were draped with white muslin, and a temple in the middle of the room held two bands, concealed behind banks of artificial flowers. Covered walks led to various supper tents, painted with allegorical subjects such as "The Overthrow of Tyranny by the Allied Military Powers."

Penelope hardly noticed any of this splendor. She was introduced to one guest after another by Lord Barrington, some she knew and some she didn't, and all the while hard eyes stared from her to her elderly escort, judging, speculating, and finding fault.

She curtsied and murmured replies — and then suddenly stood still. The Earl of Hestleton was disappearing down one of the walks.

She gave a hasty excuse and slipped away

before anyone could stop her, her heart hammering against her ribs. She went from one supper tent to another, searching among the guests, and at last she found him.

He was standing with Guy Manton and a group of friends. He looked as austere and elegant as she remembered, with only a hectic gleam in his eye betraying that he had had too much to drink. These eyes suddenly focused on Penelope as she stood shyly at the entrance to the tent, almost as if the Earl were wondering if he had seen a vision.

Penelope certainly looked ethereal enough with her slight figure trembling as she stared at him with wide, pathetic eyes.

The Earl turned to his friends and said in a loud voice, "I heard a vastly amusing song. I must sing it to you." His friends laughed and cheered him on.

To Penelope's horror, he began to sing "The Harlot's Progress" in a loud baritone. She swung round and found her way barred by Augusta, Lord Barrington, and Miss Stride who were staring at the Earl. Slowly she turned around again and faced the Earl.

He spoke, rather than sang, the last two lines. Holding up his glass and bowing low to Penelope, he said slowly, "And now (though sad and wonderful it sounds) *I would not touch her for a hundred pounds.*"

Penelope's eyes filled with tears as the Earl handed his glass to one of his friends and strode towards her and grasped her wrist. "Tell me, my sweet," he said in a mocking voice, "who is enjoying the pink and white favors of your body now. Barrington? Ah, Barrington, I can recommend her. Extremely warm in bed and quite economical out of it. A bargain, dear boy, I can assure you."

Barrington froze and then glanced at Augusta. "What's this?" he cried. "I thought your niece a virgin. I didn't know you were trying to unload Haymarket ware onto me!"

Penelope pulled her wrist from the Earl's grasp and fled, running, stumbling, and pushing her way through the startled guests. She did not stay to collect her wrap but fled in a demented way through the dark streets. A group of wild bloods tried to block her path, but she eluded their grasping hands and stumbled onwards.

She arrived at last at Brook Street and paused for a moment, clutching the railings and holding her side, waiting to recover her breath. The butler answered her knock at the door and looked curiously at her tearstained face, but Penelope flew past him and up the stairs to her room. She hurriedly crammed her old clothes into a bandbox and then scrambled out of her court dress. She must get away before Augusta returned. She must escape in case the Earl arrived to taunt her further. She was ruined! All London would know by morning that she had slept with the Earl! "Augusta will kill me," thought poor Penelope, little realising that Augusta was actually capable of doing just that.

She did not want to take any of the dresses Augusta had given her but common sense prevailed. She took three of the plainest dresses and packed them with the old ones and then sadly put on the old gown she had worn when she had travelled to London so hopefully those few months ago.

It was then she realised she had no money. The only place she could think of to go to was back to the seminary in Bath, but she had not even a penny of her own. There was the diamond pendant, but she did not feel she could take it.

Suddenly she remembered the artist, Mr. Liwoski. He had been very kind to her and they had often chatted together when he had finished his work for the day. Augusta had his address in the drawing room bureau. She ran softly down the stairs and gently opened the drawing room door.

The Comte de Chernier rose to his feet.

Penelope gave a gasp and stared at him in dismay.

"Do not be frightened of me, Miss Vesey," said the Comte. "I am waiting your aunt's return from Clarence House. You are back early."

Penelope hardly knew the man but his voice was sympathetic and, before she could stop herself, she was pouring the whole story into his ears.

The Comte surveyed her thoughtfully. It was entirely in his own interest to have the beautiful Miss Vesey out of the way. Augusta's plans for social advancement would then only rely upon himself.

"Come, my child," he said. "I am a great friend of your aunt and you must think of me as an uncle. I am ever ready to help beauty in distress. I shall give you money, my dear, and you may make your way to this seminary in Bath. No, no! I insist." He pulled three rouleaux of guineas from a capacious pocket and put them into her hand.

"This is a fortune!" said Penelope. "I do not need all this. I only need my coach fare to Bath."

"Come now," said the Comte. "I insist. I think I hear your aunt's carriage." He thought no such thing but he was anxious to be rid of Penelope. Penelope turned white and ran to the door.

"*Au revoir!*" called the Comte after her, "*et bon voyage.*"

Penelope had only been gone a half hour before Augusta's carriage rattled to a halt outside.

She waddled into the drawing room and stopped short at the sight of the Comte. "Where is she?" she snarled.

"Penelope?" said the Comte, raising his thin brows. "Your niece has left, madam. She said something incoherent about throwing herself in the river."

"Good riddance," said Augusta, sitting down heavily.

"She'd bedded with Hestleton which would have been all right had she kept him engaged to her. But she didn't. So she's labelled a tart.

"Had she still been here, I would have whipped that slut within an inch of her life. Barrington called me a Covent Garden Abbess. Said I had been trying to foist a shopworn slut onto him. Was there ever such a night!"

"It looks as if you will need me more than ever," murmured the Comte, but Augusta was still reliving the humiliations of the evening.

"And if that weren't enough," she went on, "Hestleton starts sneering at me in front of everyone. Called me the pig-faced lady and said it was the first time he had seen a sow crossed with a mushroom."

The Comte raised his hand to hide a smile. "Never mind," he said, "if you continue your work, you will soon have your title."

"I want it in writing," said Augusta.

"Come now, madam, you cannot expect me to commit myself on paper."

Augusta looked at him, her eyes suddenly gleaming with triumph as she remembered that her evening at Clarence House had not been a total disaster.

"Oh, yes you will," she said. "Would it interest you to know that I was hidden in a certain antechamber when the Duke of Wellington and the Prince Regent were having a certain private discussion?"

The Comte surveyed her for a long minute. Then he rose and walked to a desk and pulled the inkstand towards him.

"As you will, dear Miss Harvey," he said over his shoulder. "What an enterprising lady you are, to be sure.

"But I pray you, send me no more pickled bodies. It quite upsets my digestion. I have not drunk a glass of canary since!"

★ ★ ★

While Augusta and the Comte bargained, Penelope was lucky enough to obtain a room at the Belle Savage on Ludgate Hill. For one hundred and six shillings and three farthings, she managed to secure an inside seat in the coach which left at five o'clock in the morning.

She tossed and turned on the damp, unaired sheets of her bedchamber, waiting for the dawn, dreading that any minute the door would open and Augusta would waddle over the threshold.

Penelope was now very frightened of her aunt. If only she had left long ago. But she had hung on, hoping against hope for a reconciliation with the Earl. He had turned out to be a heartless, mocking dandy and Aunt Augusta, an evil, callous woman. As a rosy dawn sent long fingers into the dingy room, Penelope's despair and misery began to flee before an overpowering hate for the Earl.

He had not wanted to marry her after all! He had become engaged to her only to trick her into his bed, and, having done so, had no more use for her.

She would pay back the Comte every penny he had given her. There, at least, was one gentleman!

By the time Penelope had dressed and

washed, eaten a surprisingly good breakfast, and climbed into the coach, her youthful optimism had begun to rise to the surface. Life at the seminary would be hard, but after a few months she would ask the Misses Fry to find her a position as a governess.

For three long days the milestones passed Penelope's unseeing eyes — Hounslow, Windsor, Maidenhead, Reading, Newbury, Marlborough, Chippenham, and so to Bath.

Penelope dismounted stiffly at the White Lion. She was too anxious about her future to wait there for breakfast but immediately hired a hack to take her to the seminary.

How dark and dingy it looked, she thought as she paid off the hack and pushed open the tall wrought-iron gates.

The tall, thin house had a silent, brooding air and an unseasonal chill wind was blowing from the crescent of hills which surrounds the city of Bath.

Penelope rapped on the knocker and waited. The door opened a crack and the sleepy face of little Mary, the scullery maid, peered out through the opening.

"Oh, miss!" cried Mary, opening the door wide. "Have you come to take me away? Remember as how you said I could be your lady's maid." Mary's voice faltered as she noticed Penelope's old dress and shabby bonnet.

"I'm sorry, Mary," said Penelope gently. "I have come back to try to find work. Things did not work out at all as we hoped."

"Oh, you poor lamb," cried Mary, pulling her into the house. "The dragons isn't awake yet, only me, so come down to the kitchen and I'll brew us a nice cup of tea."

Penelope wearily followed the little scullery maid down the stairs. She suddenly felt very tired indeed.

"The Misses Fry was ever so proud of you," said Mary, pouring boiling water into a teapot. "They saw your engagement to that Earl in the *Court Circular* and showed it all round the school . They . . ."

"*Mary,*" came a stern voice from the doorway. Miss Harriet Fry stood there, her curl papers bristling. "That tea is *not* for the servants." She suddenly caught sight of Penelope.

"Miss Vesey," she cried. "How nice of you to pay us a visit."

Penelope got to her feet and Miss Harriet's quick eyes took note of her shabby appearance and her face hardened.

"I — I am actually come on a matter of business."

"In*deed!*" said Miss Harriet majestically.

163

"Then please follow me to the study. I will speak to you later, Mary."

Penelope followed the stout little figure of Miss Harriet up the familiar steps and into the study. She had a desolate feeling of once more being under authority.

"Well, Miss Vesey?" said Harriet, sitting down and addressing herself to the fire irons. She did not ask Penelope to sit.

"My visit to my aunt was not successful," said Penelope, "and I wondered if you would consider employing me as a governess?"

"You were engaged to the Earl of Hestleton," exclaimed Miss Harriet. "We read it in the *Court Circular.* What happened?"

"The Earl and I decided we should not suit," said Penelope quietly.

Miss Harriet arose and addressed herself to the clock on the mantelpiece. "We have no vacancies, Miss Vesey. Had we not just employed a music teacher — a singularly charming man and distantly related to the Smythe-Bellings — perhaps we might have seen our way to taking you back. But as it is . . ." Her voice trailed off.

Penelope picked up the rags of her dignity along with her bandbox. "Perhaps then," she suggested, "you could recommend me for a post as governess in some household?"

"Oh, no, no. I couldn't do that," said Miss Harriet to the carpet. "After all, there's something havey-cavey about your return from London. If you did not suit such a lady as Miss Harvey — seventy-five thousand a year, charming! — there must be some *flaw* in your character. You *do* understand?"

"Oh, yes, I understand," said Penelope. "You could very well help me, but humiliating me seems to be infinitely more enjoyable. Good day to you, ma'am."

Penelope left before Miss Harriet could think of a rejoinder.

As she marched to the gate, she heard the light patter of footsteps behind her and swung around. It was little Mary, her eyes wide with concern. "Oh, miss," she gasped, "wouldn't they take you back?"

Penelope shook her head and then, searching in her reticule, found two guineas and pressed them into Mary's work-worn hand. "There you are, Mary," said Penelope, fighting back tears, "that will at least buy you some cakes." And she walked hurriedly out through the gates and off down the road, leaving Mary standing in the driveway, staring at the gold.

A pale small sun had risen on a gusty, blustery day with great white castles of clouds sweeping over the hills. Penelope turned a bend in the road and when she was sure she was at last out of sight of the windows of the seminary, she sat down on a grassy bank beside the road and cried and cried. Cried for her lost love; cried because people were never what they seemed, and for the bitter end of her cherished dream of a home of her own.

She was so engrossed in her misery that she did not hear the heavy rumbling of wheels or notice the antiquated travelling carriage rounding the bend.

The carriage lurched to a stop beside her, and a woman's fat jolly face in an enormous poke bonnet peered out of the window.

Penelope suddenly noticed the coach and the fact that the carriage door was opening and fumbled for her handkerchief.

She looked slowly up. A large motherly woman was standing in front of her. "You're in trouble," said the lady. "Mr. Jennings saw you first. He's got quick eyes and he says, 'Mrs. Jennings,' he says, 'there's a young miss in trouble. Get down instanter and see if you can help.' So here I am."

"I-I'm qu-quite all right," stammered Penelope. "I-I h-have something in m-my eye."

"Well, it stands to reason you wouldn't

want to confide in a stranger," said Penelope's companion, "but you can't sit here by the road. You come with us to the nearest inn for we're both in need of a luncheon and perhaps you'll feel better when you have had some food."

Penelope suddenly realised she was very hungry indeed and, apart from that, she no longer cared much what happened to her so she allowed herself to be led into the coach.

Her newfound friends kept a tactful silence until they were all seated round a table in the upstairs parlor of the nearest hostelry.

Mr. Jennings was a complete contrast to his buxom, jolly wife. He was a thin, ascetic gentleman with a dry, scholarly voice. He refused to let Penelope speak until she had eaten a substantial meal, conversing instead with his garrulous wife. Penelope gathered that the couple was setting out from Bath on the long journey to their home in Dover. Mr. Jennings had been taking the waters at Bath for a liver complaint. The visit to Bath had effected a cure, caused, claimed Mr. Jennings, by the rest from work and strict diet rather than by the sulphurous waters of Bath.

When the covers were finally removed, he called for a churchwarden, and once the long clay pipe had been lit, turned to

Penelope and asked her in his dry, precise voice if there was any way in which he could be of service to her.

The former sparkling innocence of Penelope's blue eyes had fled to be replaced by a wary, hurt look. The Jenningses seemed kind, but who could tell? Perhaps they had hopes of marrying her off to the richest man in Dover to further their social ambitions!

Nonetheless she related baldly, in a tired little voice, that she had been seeking her former employment at the Misses Fry's seminary, without success. She made no mention of the Earl, only stating that she was returning to Bath after a brief stay with her aunt in London. She and her aunt had had a certain disagreement. No, she had no other relatives or friends who would aid her. She thanked them for their hospitality but insisted she must be on her way.

"Oh, but . . ." burst out Mrs. Jennings and was silenced by a look from her more phlegmatic husband.

"Now, Miss Vesey," he said, puffing on his long pipe. "It so happens that we can help you. We have two daughters, Jane and Alice, who are at a seminary in Dover. They are just finishing but are in need of some town bronze before their come out. Nothing very grand, you understand. They will only be attending the local assemblies and parties. I am a lawyer by profession and we do not move much in very elevated society.

"My wife is kept too busy to train the girls herself. She . . ."

"Come now," interrupted his wife with a jolly laugh. "You know well, Mr. Jennings, that I'm too rough and ready. I'm all thumbs in grand society."

"But with a very beautiful soul," said Mr. Jennings simply, and his wife blushed like a girl.

Why, they are in love! thought Penelope in wonder. Love in London society seemed to be an exclusively extramarital emotion.

"In any case, Miss Vesey," went on the lawyer in his dry, precise voice, "I would have you understand I am not offering you charity. We are in need of a governess to train our girls in the social arts. As I say, we are not very grand people but my wife runs a comfortable home. I shall give you a few minutes to think about it."

Penelope did not need long to ponder her answer. She simply had nowhere else to go.

Soon the Jenningses' coach rolled away from the inn, down the dusty road on the first part of the long journey south, taking Penelope with it to a new and unknown home.

Chapter Eleven

Augusta Harvey was suffering from the full weight of the Earl of Hestleton's dislike. With his patronage removed, society discovered that Augusta was as common as they had formerly thought.

Since that fatal evening at Clarence House, no cards had arrived at Brook Street and there were no more homes of the powerful and influential for Augusta to snoop around.

She had paid a visit to the Comte in Barnet, only to find that gentleman engaged in his packing. In a panic Augusta had insisted that the Comte take her to France with him.

"But Napoleon is, alas, still on Elba," the Comte had said. "I fear you are premature."

"I'm going," Augusta had said mulishly. "I ain't staying here after all my work for France to be snubbed at and jeered at. You're taking me along."

The Comte had at last wearily agreed.

There was a certain Captain Jessey, he had said, whose ship, the *Mary Jane*, would drop them on the coast of France. Augusta must make her own way to Dover and he would meet her at the Green Man inn and then they would make their way to the ship together.

After all, the Comte had reflected, a little more money and the obliging Captain Jessey would make sure that Miss Harvey fell over the side of his ship before it reached the other side of the Channel.

He shuddered to think what Augusta would say — or do — should she find that there was as little chance of her becoming a Countess in France as there was in England, or that the Bonapartistes had never even heard of Augusta, the Comte having taken the full credit for all of Augusta's information. Augusta, on her last visit to France, had been hoodwinked by a visit to a chateau in the Loire valley — empty except for the heavily bribed servants. She had spent a pleasant day touring what she believed to be her future estates.

Now Augusta was sitting among her corded trunks, awaiting the arrival of the travelling coach she had hired. She thanked her lucky stars for the day she had overheard the Comte and the Viscount talking.

Without her promise of a French title, then life would be bitter indeed. What a waste of time and money that little slut Penelope had been! Fortunately the magnificent diamond pendant Lord Barrington had given Penelope had more than covered the expense of that girl's wardrobe. Who would have thought that Penelope with all her airs and graces would have fallen so easily from her pedestal of virginity!

She looked up in impatience as Miss Stride was announced. Miss Stride had two angry spots of color burning on her cheeks which owed nothing to rouge. In her hand she clutched a sheaf of bills.

"What is this, Miss Harvey?" she burst out. "My mantua maker has returned these bills to me saying that you have refused to honor them."

"Quite right," said Augusta.

"How dare you!" said Miss Stride, beginning to tremble with rage. "The humiliation! And after all I've done for you."

"You! What have you ever done for me, except teach me not to eat peas with my knife?" sneered Augusta. "When Hestleton took agin me, there was nothing you could do, Euphie, for all your airs and graces."

"If you will give me some time . . ." began Miss Stride, cracks beginning to show in her new veneer of assertion.

"I ain't got the time," said Augusta. "I'm taking a trip to France and I won't be back for a long time."

"But I have no money," wailed Euphemia Stride. "You have furthermore encouraged me to run up these bills and although several of them may be in my name, I would remind you they were gowns ordered for you."

"Then it might teach you a bit of worldly wisdom," laughed Augusta. She suddenly pushed her large face towards the spinster.

"Lookee here, Euphie," she said. "You've simpered and talked of the importance of having aristocratic connections and a good name. Well, then, I suggest you take your good name and go and live off somebody else. Remember, the good Lord says that unto them that hath, shall be given, an' I hath, Euphie, and you hathent. So there!"

"You're heartless," said Miss Stride, beginning to cry. "You don't even care what became of that niece of yours."

"No, I don't. Any more than I care what happens to you," said Augusta with her smile at its widest. "You see, it all comes of being too trusting. Now I — I am *never* trusting. Look at that idiot Penelope. She needs must go and fall in love with Hestleton and so she ends up in the gutter.

Anyway, he didn't drop Penelope 'cause she had a bit of a roll in the hay with him. It was all on account of that brother of his, dying like that."

"But it was a seizure," gasped Miss Stride, momentarily diverted from her own troubles.

"Ho! That was no seizure. Why, that silly Charles takes a pistol and blows his brains out and he leaves this silly letter . . ." Augusta bit her fat lip and her protruding eyes bulged from her head in alarm. She had nearly gone too far.

"What were you about to say?" said Miss Stride sharply.

"Nothing," muttered Augusta.

"You had something to do with Charles's death," said Miss Stride, her voice suddenly becoming stronger. "Pay these bills, Augusta, or I shall . . . I shall . . ."

"You'll what?"

"I'll . . . I'll go straight to the Earl of Hestleton and tell him what you told me!"

"Go ahead," said Augusta with massive indifference, "I won't be around when his lordship comes calling."

"You'd better not," said Euphemia Stride as she turned towards the door, "because I am going right to the Earl this minute and . . . and . . . don't *ever* come back to London again, Augusta, or it will be the worse for you."

"Get out of here before I kill you," said Augusta quietly.

Miss Stride looked at her ex-patroness, and what she saw in Augusta's green eyes made her pick up her skirts with a squeak of alarm and run from the house.

Rourke, the butler, looked disapprovingly at the flustered spinster standing in the Earl's hallway. A lady like Miss Stride, he thought, should know better than to go calling on a gentleman in his town house.

"But it is very important," Miss Stride was insisting. "I have news for my lord concerning Miss Vesey."

"In that case," said Rourke, his face hardening, "my lord is most definitely not at home."

"What is it, Rourke?"

The butler and Miss Stride swung round. The Earl was standing at the top of the stairs, dressed to go out. Miss Stride scurried round the butler. "My lord," she called, "my lord! 'Tis vastly important. I have news of Miss Vesey."

A shutter seemed to close down over the Earl's face. He descended the stairs slowly, drawing on his driving gloves. "I am going out, Miss Stride," he said in a flat voice. "I beg you to excuse me."

"But Penelope . . ."

Rourke was already holding up the Earl's many-caped driving coat.

"But it also concerns your brother," wailed Miss Stride. "About that letter . . . and about Charles shooting himself."

The Earl paused, frozen, one arm in the sleeve of his coat. Rourke's face was like wood.

The Earl slowly withdrew his arm.

"Follow me, Miss Stride," he said abruptly and led the way upstairs to his private sitting room.

Miss Stride followed him in and sat down on the edge of a rope-backed chair. The Earl looked very grim. She began to wish she had not come.

"Very well," said the Earl, sitting down opposite her. "Proceed!"

"Well . . . well . . ." faltered Miss Stride. "It's like this."

She told the Earl Augusta's strange remarks about Charles's death and the letter, ending up with the outburst of, "Augusta's a wicked woman. She has no delicacy, no *feeling*. She even sneered at poor Penelope for having fallen in love with you . . ."

Miss Stride broke off. The Earl's eyes had

the hard, silver shine of mercury. "I'll kill her," grated the Earl, and Miss Stride realised with a gasp of relief that his rage was directed toward Augusta and not herself.

"Where is Miss Vesey now?" demanded the Earl.

"I-I d-don't know," stammered Miss Stride. "She disappeared after the Clarence House ball. She had no money, not a penny. She did not even take the diamond pendant that my Lord Barrington had given her. I have no money, my lord, or I would endeavour to find her whereabouts."

"You can have all my money an' you find Miss Vesey," said the Earl grimly, well aware that the spinster lived on her wits.

Hope activated Miss Stride's nimble brain. "Perhaps Miss Vesey has returned to the seminary in Bath, though she would have had to walk. Perhaps I could travel there myself . . ."

"I will go," said the Earl. He crossed to his desk and scribbled rapidly. "There you are, Miss Stride — a draft on my bank and thank you for your information. I shall call on Miss Harvey first."

Miss Stride carefully deposited the draft in her reticule before she spoke. "I fear Miss Harvey has already left," she said. "She said she was leaving for France."

"Then after I have found Miss Vesey's whereabouts," said the Earl, "I shall follow Miss Harvey to France and personally wring her fat neck. You may go, Miss Stride." He tugged at the bell, but Miss Stride would not even wait for the servant. She fled from the room.

Outside she paused and took a deep breath and then slowly drew the Earl's note from her reticule and blinked at the enormous sum. Euphemia Stride's troubles and woes fled like magic to be replaced by a fierce gratitude. She would repay the Earl, who was obviously still in love with Penelope. Then, she, Euphemia Stride would help the couple in the only way she could. She would use her busy tongue to tell the *ton* that Penelope Vesey had been grossly misjudged, rouse their wrath against Augusta, and make sure that should Miss Vesey return to London, society would at least have a welcome for her.

The Earl sat in silence after she had left, his mind racing. He was suddenly sure that Penelope had had nothing to do with the blackmailing of Charles. He should have known all along, but the shock of his brother's death had turned his mind. He groaned aloud. He was as bad as Augusta. And Augusta had said that Penelope had loved him! In his bitterness and hate, in his misguided attempts to save his brother's name, he had condemned the only girl he had ever really loved . . . to what?

He suddenly sprang to his feet and, calling loudly for his racing curricle to be brought round from the stables, started to make hasty preparations for a journey to Bath. Augusta Harvey could await his vengeance. The most important thing was to find Penelope. Whatever had become of her?

Penelope had survived, although at times the Jennings had feared she would not. After the rigors of the journey to the Jenningses' comfortable home in the small village of Wold outside Dover, after the settling in, after the introductions to Mr. Jennings's two buxom daughters, Penelope had suddenly collapsed from delayed shock. Up till then the need to survive had sustained her. But in the relaxing and comfortable atmosphere of the Jenningses' home all the memories had come tumbling back. As she tossed and turned at night, the Earl's voice sneered along the corridors of her dreams, "I would not touch her for a hundred pounds."

The fact that she had lost her virginity to a heartless rake and had been also duped by her hard and grasping aunt made her alternately boil and burn with shame and hate. Added to that was the awful fear that she might have become pregnant and surely even the kindly Jenningses would have thrown her out of doors should that have happened. Her temperature rose alarmingly and she spent her first week at the Jenningses turning and tossing in fevered coma.

At last the fever had broken. With it had come the knowledge that she was going to live after all. Penelope had shakily started to put her mind and her world together again. Gradually she began to work at her duties as governess.

Jane and Alice Jennings did not seem overly interested in learning the hows and wherefores of social behavior. They were jolly country girls, very like their mother. But they enjoyed Penelope's company on their walks and shopping expeditions and tried very hard to become fashionable young ladies to please her.

It was, surprisingly, their mother, the noisy, garrulous Mrs. Jennings, who became Penelope's most successful pupil — although not in the arts of social behavior. Mrs. Jennings turned out to have a great love of music and was never happier than when Penelope was giving her lessons on the pianoforte or listening to Penelope playing in the long, dark autumn evenings when chill winds blew across the English Channel and great waves pounded at the foot of the chalky cliffs.

Penelope was able to lose herself in her music and find some relief from her painful memories.

The Jenningses' house was a square barracks of a place, built of gray stone, standing four square near the edge of the cliffs and surrounded by a neat and formal garden. The furniture was old-fashioned and the floors were uncarpeted, but the Jenningses went in for roaring fires and great, satisfying meals so that the house was always redolent of the smells of woodsmoke and good country cooking.

Local village society seemed to be limited to that of the schoolmaster and his large, noisy family of small children and to the vicar and his shy, little wife. Jane and Alice would often stop in the village street to giggle and laugh with the farmers' sons, and Penelope often thought that they would make excellent farmers' wives, being more interested in the friendly camaraderie of the farming families and crops and cattle than they were in preparing for the parties and balls in nearby Dover.

One day Mr. Jennings proposed that Penelope should escort the girls into Dover on a shopping expedition. She was to spend the afternoon with them in the town and then take them for tea to the Green Man which was famous for its cakes and pastries and then bring them home before dark.

The day was fine when they set out, a great pale yellow sun glittering and shining on the frosty fields and bare, skeletal branches of the trees. Penelope observed to the Jenningses' coachman, John, that it was fine weather, to which John eyed the sky uneasily and said it was "too bright."

"What do you mean?" laughed Penelope. "Surely in England the sun can never be too bright!"

John scratched his powdered hair. "Well, it's like this, miss," he said. "When the sun is all shiny and glittery like that, usually it means we're going to get a powerful bit of wind."

"Nonsense!" teased Penelope. "You've been reading your almanack again, John. Why, there's not a breath of wind!"

Certainly it continued fine as the carriage lumbered onto the turnpike road and started the six-mile descent to Dover with a series of chalk cliffs and the blue sea on the right and, on the left, the bare winter brown of the cornfields.

Before they reached the town of Dover, Penelope glanced once more out to sea. The sky still stretched blue and cloudless as far as the eye could see, but the sea appeared to have abruptly changed to a gray metallic color which seemed to change to black, even as she looked.

She pointed this phenomenon out to John, sticking her head out of the open carriage window and calling up to him as he sat majestically on his box.

John promptly reined in his horses. "It's like I told you, miss," he said, twisting round on the box to look down at Penelope. "Storm's a-coming. We'd best go back."

"Oh, *no!*" screamed Jane and Alice in unison, their black ringlets bobbing. "Miss Vesey, tell him we *must* go on."

"Very well," smiled Penelope, amused at the girls' enthusiasm for shopping, little realising that Jane and Alice had heard that Farmer Galt's sons were visiting Dover and that they hoped to see them.

Jane and Alice were dressed alike. Their warm pelisses and velvet dresses were of different colors, eighteen-year-old Jane being in blue and seventeen-year-old Alice in scarlet, but they were so alike in character that somehow they always *looked* as if they

183

were dressed the same. Both were buxom, both had rosy cheeks. Jane had smaller eyes and a longer nose than her sister, but that seemed to be the only difference.

"Perhaps we shall find a beau for you, Miss Vesey?" teased Jane. "You are so pretty, it seems a shame you are not married."

"I shall never marry," said Penelope in a quiet voice, and both her charges fell silent, remembering their mother's speculations that Miss Vesey was suffering from a broken heart.

The sun was still bathing the cobbles of Dover in a warm, pale golden light when Penelope and the girls alighted from the carriage. But John, the coachman, was still muttering and prophesying bad weather, and after Penelope and her charges had left to look at the shops, he drove to the Green Man and bespoke rooms for all them for the night. He had a strong feeling in his rheumaticky bones that they would not be returning home that day.

The town of Dover was very like other English seaport towns except that it was cleaner and had fewer ruffians hanging about. Penelope found it a very picturesque place. On one side of the town the old castle was perched on the top of a very steep hill.

On the other side was a great chalk hill, very nearly perpendicular, rising up from sixty to a hundred feet higher than the tops of the houses which huddled at the foot of the hill. Penelope was amazed to see cows grazing on a spot apparently fifty feet above the tops of the houses and measuring horizontally not more than twenty feet.

It made the perspective look excitingly and magically wrong somehow — like the perspectives in some early paintings. On the south side of the town stood the cliff described by Shakespeare in *King Lear*:

How fearful
And dizzy 'tis to cast one's eyes so low!
The crows and choughs that wing the
    midway air
Show scarce so gross as beetles: half way
    down
Hangs one that gathers samphire,
    dreadful trade!
Methinks he seems no bigger than his
    head . . .

On a previous visit Penelope had stood on the cliff, watching the men gathering plants below and had then retreated quickly from the edge of the cliff, almost overcome with dizziness. It had not changed at all since

Shakespeare's day. She envied the cows and sheep that grazed, unconcerned, at the very edge of the cliff as if they were browsing in some placid valley.

Penelope ushered the girls into Mr. Jobbin's in the high street — to buy green tea on the one side of the shop and to examine silk ribbons on the other. The shop was pretty well filled. Shy farmers stood around the grocery counter, slicking down their hair and looking nervously out of the sides of their eyes at Mr. Jobbin's smart young assistants who had on very fashionable cravats and leaped backwards and forwards over the counters, vaulting with amazing dexterity, their coattails flying behind them.

Penelope had taken to wearing caps which she felt suitable to her governess position. While the girls were looking through a box of ribbons, Penelope bought herself a new cap and stood back to wait until the girls were finished. It was then, as their plump gloved hands turned over the silk ribbons, that Penelope saw a flash of gold-colored ribbon. All at once she was transported back in her mind to that night at Almack's where she had worn the dress with the gold ribbons. She felt suddenly weak and faint and looked wildly round until she found a chair to sit down on. Gradually the faintness receded. She arose unsteadily and went to the silk counter to fetch her charges, but of Jane and Alice there was no sign.

Thoroughly worried and harassed, Penelope asked the stately Mr. Jobbin himself if he had seen the girls. "I saw them stepping out just some minutes ago, ma'am," said Mr. Jobbin with a low bow. "They said something to me about getting some fresh air and that they would be meeting you at the Green Man for tea."

"*Oh!*" said Penelope with a mixture of amusement and exasperation. "I believe the girls have gone to look for something less salubrious than fresh air."

Now, thought Penelope, standing outside the shop, if I were making an assignation, where should I go? The quay, that was it!

As she walked down the steep hill towards the quay, she suddenly realised that great black clouds were massing on the horizon and a blustery wind had begun to blow from the sea. The tall, thin masts of the ships were bobbing and swaying as if some winter forest had come to life.

It did not take her long to spy the buxom figures of her charges, giggling and laughing with Farmer Galt's sons.

Her charges accepted her rebuke with

their customary good humor while the Galt brothers grinned and looked sheepish.

Penelope marched the girls up the windy hill to the Green Man. The wind was now blowing with full force and as they came in sight of the inn, an icy squall of rain struck them and sent them scurrying for shelter.

John was lounging at the entrance to the inn with a satisfied I-told-you-so look on his face.

"We'll not get home to Wold," he told Penelope with obvious satisfaction. "I took the liberty of bespeaking rooms for you and the Misses Jennings. Also a snug private parlor."

Penelope could only thank him as she looked back at the rain-drenched street and up at the sky which was now boiling black above the town.

By the time she and the girls were sitting over a substantial tea in their parlor, the rain was already changing to snow. Sea and town were blotted out as great sheets of snow roared in from the Channel.

After tea she kept the girls amused with endless games of spillikins until it was time for dinner and then, after dinner, ordered them to bed.

But Penelope could not sleep. The snow changed to stabbing arrows of ice which rattled ferociously against the leaded windows. The old inn creaked and struggled in the grasp of the storm and the bed candle's flame wavered and danced in a multitude of scurrying drafts. The images of the Earl and Augusta and Charles danced in the black corners of the room.

She thought for the hundredth time of the bitter complexities of the human character where a seemingly fastidious and honorable man such as the Earl, who had held her so passionately in his arms and promised her the world and all, should underneath be a weak and vicious philanderer.

She could not help wondering if he ever thought of her at all, and groaned as she thought that at that very moment some other naïve debutante might be trembling in his arms and listening to all those speeches of love which she had trustingly believed had been for her alone.

But there was no female present to console the unhappy and dispirited Earl who had returned from a fruitless visit to Bath. He had eased his feelings by giving the Misses Fry a piece of his mind, but now he did not know what to do.

He was roused from his depression by his butler, Rourke, who entered the room and stood before him, looking shaken and nervous and not at all like his usual calm and urbane self.

"What is it, Rourke?" asked the Earl testily.

"I have betrayed you!" cried Rourke. "Oh, my lord, forgive me. It was the Fatal Tendency."

"What are you talking about, man?"

"I gave you my solemn promise not to reveal the particulars of Lord Charles's death," said Rourke in a shaky voice, "but I failed you. A certain young footman called Snyle knew of my weakness for drink and filled me full of ale, plying me with questions the while. I had no recollection of telling him anything.

"But Miss Harvey's house is in an uproar. She has gone off to Dover to take a ship for France. She told the servants she was taking a short holiday, but it appears she has sold the house and left them without their wages. When I was talking to them, I learned that Snyle had been in her employ and had mysteriously disappeared on the day after I had been drinking with him. Well, Snyle had let several hints drop in the servants' hall that he intended to make his fortune by finding out information about Lord Charles's death. I cannot remember but I feel I must have let something fall when I was in my cups. Oh, my lord. I feel you can never forgive me!"

"Dover," said the Earl, his face white and set. "I tell you, Rourke, you shall easily repair any damage you have done by serving me in this way. You shall accompany me to Dover and aid me in hunting down Augusta Harvey. Our name is worth nothing should this traitor go free . . . for I feel sure Augusta is a traitor.

"The roads will be bad, so we will need to ride. Have four of our best mounts saddled up and we shall take with us two of the burliest footmen. Now, bustle about man! We are no longer interested in the damage that has been done but how we can best mend matters. Mayhap Augusta knows the direction of her niece and I shall choke that information out of her — before I kill her!"

Penelope gave up trying to sleep. Her thoughts were too anguished and the noise of the storm too loud. She decided to go along the corridor and make sure that the girls were safely tucked up.

She put on her wrap and picked up her bed candle and quietly opened the door. The narrow corridor was very dim, lit only by the light of a small oil lamp hanging from a bracket on the wall halfway along. Then she heard the sound of another door being opened and drew back into the doorway of her own bedroom, not wanting to run into another guest while she was in her night attire. She cautiously peered round the doorjamb and then stood rigid, the candlestick tilting dangerously in her trembling hand. Augusta Harvey came quietly out of a room, went a little way down the corridor, and vanished into a room at the end.

"I'm going mad!" thought Penelope wildly. "My nightmares are coming true!"

But an innate common sense told her terrified brain that what she had seen was a real-live person. Like a sleepwalker, Penelope moved along the corridor until she reached the door through which Augusta Harvey had just disappeared.

"Well, what news?" came the unmistakable harsh voice of Augusta.

To Penelope's surprise another voice she recognised answered her aunt.

"We shall not be sailing tonight, Miss Harvey. The storm is too fierce and Captain Jessey says it may be a few days before we have a fair wind for France."

It was the Comte!

Penelope stayed rooted to the spot, almost leaning against the door, although the voices carried easily above the roar of the storm.

"Gad's 'oonds!" said Augusta furiously. "I feel like a trapped rat! What if Hestleton should have changed his mind and come looking for me!"

"Hestleton is too proud," replied the Comte in his familiar sibilant tones. "He will do all in his power not to besmirch his family escutcheon. He would not have it known that his young brother blew his brains out because he was a Bonapartiste spy. Which reminds me, you played your cards wrong over that little affair."

"How so?" snarled Augusta.

"Well, when you had found out from the late and unlamented Snyle that Lord Charles had left a letter explaining that you had been blackmailing him so that he would introduce Penelope to his brother in the hope that the Earl would marry her, the Earl naturally thought Penelope was part of the blackmailing scheme.

"Now, had you convinced him she was not, I feel sure he would still have married her because, if ever I saw a man head over heels in love, that was the Earl."

"Oh, I knew that," said Augusta impatiently.

"Then why . . . ?"

"Because," said Augusta patiently while Penelope's poor heart and mind seemed to be doing somersaults, "he would have married her, but I would have never been allowed to set foot in any of his households and the only reason I wanted that little baggage to marry him was to afford me a social entrée. Why should I spend money on her and not benefit myself, heh!"

Penelope leaned forward and pressed her ear against the door. She must write to the Earl, she must tell him all she could find out.

The Comte's voice came again, sounding faintly amused. "Dear Miss Harvey, you are always describing the horrors of hellfire so accurately. Do you never fear them yourself? After all, you are a murderess, a poisoner, in fact — *hélas,* poor Snyle, I knew him well — a traitor, and, who knows, perhaps a double murderess if the luckless Penelope should starve."

"I do what is right," came Augusta's sulky voice, while Penelope's brain reeled under the onslaught of this most recent information. "I wreak vengeance in His name. Yea, verily, I come with a sword . . ."

"It was rat poison in poor Snyle's case," said the Comte, sounding much amused. "Dear Miss Harvey, you are an original.

And while we're on the subject of originals, may I have my snuffbox back? The one you have just slipped into your reticule? Ah, I thank you. Now, let us have some wine and relax. Nothing can be achieved by worrying . . ."

Penelope crept off down the corridor and into the safety of her room. Her heart felt as if it were about to burst through her throat.

She sat down shakily on the edge of her bed, her thoughts as wild as the storm outside. Even the Comte, whom she had believed to be a kindly man, had turned out to be Augusta's accomplice.

She was very shocked and very afraid, but somewhere in all the confusion was a small kernel of comfort. She knew now why the Earl had behaved so.

After sleepless hours of thought she made up her mind. She would send an express to the Earl, telling him about Augusta. He would somehow know what to do. She would send the girls back home in the morning and somehow manage to stay at the inn without Augusta seeing her. If Augusta was about to set sail and the Earl had not arrived, then she, Penelope, would have to stop her somehow.

In the morning the sky was still steel gray,

but the snow which had changed to rain during the night had ceased to fall.

Penelope told the puzzled Jennings girls that she had to remain in Dover on urgent business and scurried back to the safety of her room as soon as the Jenningses' cumbersome carriage had rolled out of sight.

Now all she had to do was wait . . .

Chapter Twelve

Two days later, Penelope was still fretting in her room. The wind had died down and the sky was clear but the sea was still stormy with tall white-capped waves churning across its surface.

It was late afternoon and the light was already fading and Penelope had resigned herself to another long night's vigil, when she heard the sound of voices in the corridor. The Comte and Augusta!

She pressed her ear against the panel of the door and listened. "Then it appears we may sail tonight?" Augusta was saying.

"We may have to pay the good Captain more," the Comte replied. "I fear that . . ." But whatever the Comte feared was lost to Penelope's listening ears as he turned a bend in the corridor.

Penelope hurriedly donned her cloak, grateful for its concealing hood which she drew about her face. She crept to the top of the stairs and listened. The Comte and

Augusta were standing at the entrance to the inn. "I have had our trunks corded and put aboard," the Comte was saying. "So it is only a matter of getting Captain Jessey to take us on board as well."

They moved off and Penelope followed behind, keeping at a safe distance as they went down the windy hill to the quay.

The ships were still bobbing wildly at anchor. Penelope hid behind a bale of goods on the quay and peered cautiously round in time to see the Comte and Augusta boarding a schooner called the *Mary Jane*.

She waited for what seemed like a very long time, trembling with cold and excitement, and wondering what to do should the couple not return to dry land.

At last they appeared on the gangplank, looking very pleased with themselves. Behind them stood the squat figure of the Captain.

"I thank you, Captain," the Comte was saying, his voice carrying on the slight breeze. "We shall return in less than an hour with our personal belongings."

Penelope suddenly could not bear it any longer. She threw back her hood and ran forward, crying wildly, "Oh, stop them! Stop them! Traitors! Bonapartistes!"

Augusta stood stock-still, clutching the

rope rail of the gangplank. The Captain stood with his mouth open.

Several fishermen stopped working on their nets and came to stand and stare.

The Comte was the first to recover. "She's quite mad," he said loudly and clearly. He took Augusta's fat arm in a strong grip. "Come, my dear, and pay no attention to the town idiot."

"That man's a Frenchie," said one of the fishermen, a great burly fellow. "I vote we take them to the roundhouse and let them all tell their story there."

This was accepted as the judgment of Solomon by the ever-increasing crowd who advanced threateningly towards the ship.

Captain Jessey rapped out some sharp orders and his crew began to make the ship ready to set sail. The Comte nipped quickly back on board. Augusta threw one terrified look at the crowd and made to follow the Comte as the mainsail of the *Mary Jane* flapped and cracked as it slowly moved up the mast.

"No! You shan't escape!" cried Penelope, running forward and seizing hold of Augusta. Augusta struggled and punched like a fury while Penelope held on. The tone of the crowd had changed. It was only two women fighting after all, and a rare sight that was. They hung back and cheered Penelope on with all the enthusiasm of an audience at a prize fight.

Penelope's desperate cries for help were lost in the appreciative roars of the crowd.

"Either come or stay," shouted Captain Jessey to Augusta. "We're setting sail."

Suddenly a shot whistled through the shrouds of the ship and everyone froze.

"Hold hard!" called a stern voice from the hill and the watchers swung round. Penelope and Augusta released each other and stared in the direction of the voice.

The Earl of Hestleton, with Rourke and two footmen at his heels, came bounding down towards the quay. The Earl was hatless and his auburn hair gleamed like fire in the setting sun. His clothes were travel-stained and muddy, but he was an imposing figure for all that.

"Stop that woman!" he called. "She's a traitor!"

"Spies is it!" cried the Captain in alarm. He had been prepared to take Penelope's accusations as a joke, but the sight of the formidable Earl suddenly seemed to make the charges all too true.

"I'm having none o' this," said the Captain. He gave Augusta a shove which sent her tumbling down the gangplank onto the quay. A few sharp commands and his sailors hauled the gangplank on board.

Augusta stumbled to her feet and backed towards the edge of the quay before the cold anger in the Earl's face. Penelope, who had retreated to the quay at the first sight of the Earl, stood behind the reassuring bulk of Rourke.

"You are making a mistake," babbled Augusta wildly. "It's not me. It's the Comte de Chernier you want."

The Earl looked at her with disgust and loathing. Then he lowered his pistol. "Come, Miss Harvey," he said.

Augusta twisted her head. Behind her the *Mary Jane* was already some yards from the quay.

With a hoarse cry she suddenly twisted round and jumped into the water.

Everyone rushed to the edge. Augusta was bobbing on the choppy water. She had lost her turban and wig and her thin, sparse hair floated around her fat shoulders like seaweed.

"Help! For the love of God — help!" she cried to the ship in a thin, weak voice, and then her head sank under the surface.

After a few breathless seconds it appeared again. The Earl slowly raised his pistol and levelled it at Augusta's head.

"Go on, fat 'un, swim for it!" cheered the crowd, beginning to enjoy the drama immensely. Augusta saw the sun glinting on the barrel of the Earl's pistol and saw his finger tightening on the trigger. "Penelope," she wailed.

The *Mary Jane* was still close to the quay, her sails hanging idly and her sailors crowding along the rail.

Penelope stared at the Earl in horror. He could not mean to shoot Augusta in cold blood.

She darted forward and knocked his pistol in the air, jerking the Earl's finger in the trigger. The pistol went off but the ball went sailing harmlessly over Augusta's head.

The Earl turned and glared down at Penelope. "You little . . . *accomplice!*" he hissed.

"I — I'm *not!*" cried Penelope. "Did you not receive my letter?"

But the Earl, who had left London long before Penelope's letter was even due to arrive, was too angry to listen.

A roar from the crowd made him turn around.

A squally wind had suddenly filled the sails of the *Mary Jane* and swung her round while the sailors were gazing openmouthed at Augusta struggling in the water. The great schooner bore down on her and the bow hit her full in the back of the neck before she went under. The sailors leaped to the ropes, and the *Mary Jane* narrowly missed colliding with the quay. When she moved off again, there was no sign of Augusta.

"Get a move on, man," said the Comte to Captain Jessey, "or I'll tell the world about your smuggling activities."

"Smuggling is one thing. Spying's another. Can you swim?" asked the Captain mildly, rubbing the stubble on his chin.

"No, I can't," said the Comte testily. "What's that . . ."

He got no further.

With one massive blow Captain Jessey sent him sailing over the side.

The Comte struggled and choked and flailed his arms. Suddenly, like some great monster of the deep, the dead body of Augusta surfaced in front of him, her sightless gooseberry eyes staring straight at him and her mouth stretched in an awful smile.

The Comte raised his arms in panic and sank like a stone.

Mr. and Mrs. Jennings, hurrying down to the quay, stared in amazement at the scene in front of them. A crowd was slowly moving away like a theater audience leaving when the show is over, gossiping and exclaiming and heading for the nearest alehouses to discuss the drama further.

Penelope, her long blond hair blowing in the wind and her cloak billowing out around her slim body, was staring up into the face of a tall man with copper-colored hair.

Mrs. Jennings came bustling forward. "What's all this, Miss Vesey?" she demanded. "We was that worried about you, but we couldn't get into Dover sooner because of the state of the roads."

Penelope remained silent, staring up at the Earl with a pleading look on her face.

"Go, Miss Vesey," he said in a quiet voice. "Think yourself lucky I do not put a bullet through that beautiful head of yours."

Penelope opened her mouth and then closed it again. What was the use? He was determined not to believe her. And he was little better than a murderer himself. He had been going to shoot Augusta as he would have shot a mad dog.

"Thank you for coming to collect me, Mrs. Jennings," said Penelope in a low voice. "Please take me home."

"That I will," said Mrs. Jennings in a motherly voice but with a hard look at the

Earl. "Mr. Jennings, do you but stay here and find out what has been happening. I will take Miss Vesey to the Green Man for some refreshment."

Without another look at the Earl, Penelope allowed herself to be led away.

"Now, sir," began Mr. Jennings.

But the Earl replied before he could go on, "I have no intention of giving you any explanation, sir, whoever you are. Miss Vesey may tell you what she pleases. And, now, if you will excuse me, I will go in search of the local magistrate. It is as well I go in search of him, before he comes in search of me. Good day to you!"

An hour later the Jenningses were sitting in the inn parlor and listening openmouthed to Penelope's tale of blackmail and murder and treason.

"And he's no better than my aunt," ended Penelope. "The Earl of Hestleton, I mean. He was going to kill her!"

"Brute!" said Mrs. Jennings stoutly.

Mr. Jennings put his chalky fingernails together and said in his dry, precise voice, "Now, ladies, all throughout this tale it appears to me that Miss Vesey and the Earl have let emotion take over from intellect. First, let us look at the case from the Earl's point of view. He could not possibly have received your letter before he set out from London, Miss Vesey. He finds out that the woman who drove his brother to suicide is also a traitor. He decides to no longer worry about protecting his dead brother's name — a very difficult thing for the Earl to do — supposing he is only half as proud as the gossips say he is.

"And what does he see when he arrives on the quay? You, Miss Vesey, with the conspirators."

"But he saw me fighting with my aunt!"

"Let me finish," said Mr. Jennings mildly. "The Earl is almost mad with rage. I do not believe he would actually have pulled the trigger, but, if he had, I should not have blamed him. But you, Miss Vesey, knock up his pistol, setting it off. So what does he think? He forgets about your struggles with your aunt and naturally assumes you are an accomplice.

"Now, if you and Mrs. Jennings will travel back to Wold, I will seek out the magistrate and explain your side of the business to the Earl."

"Don't," said Penelope in a low voice. "I hate him!"

Mr. Jennings sighed. "What an emotional pair of young people you are, to be sure! Each one hates the other so violently for not being perfect! Ah, well, nonetheless I must go to the magistrate. For if I do not give you some protection, Miss Vesey, the Runners may come looking for you!"

When Mr. Jennings had left, Mrs. Jennings looked anxiously at Penelope. "Why don't you have a good cry, my love," she said soothingly.

"I shall never cry over that man again!" said Penelope.

And with that, she put her head down on Mrs. Jennings's comfortable bosom and cried as if her heart would break.

Chapter Thirteen

The Earl rode up the long driveway towards Wyndham Court, failing, for the first time, to acknowledge the salute of his lodgekeeper.

He wanted to get home and bar the doors, he wanted to get drunk, he never wanted to see another woman again, he did not know *what* he wanted.

By the time he had changed out of his travel-stained clothes and was seated in front of a roaring fire in his drawing room with a glass of brandy in his hand, he began to breathe easier for the first time in days.

He had laid the whole story in front of the magistrates, nobly absolving that baggage Penelope from all blame. He had then ridden weary days to London and had put the matter before several severe gentlemen at the Foreign Office.

It was decided after much long and weary consultation and interrogation that very little harm had been done. The spies were dead and there was no reason to alarm the

British public by broadcasting Viscount Charles's part in the affair. The Foreign Office knew from their own spies in France that even that famous conversation between the Duke of Wellington and the Prince Regent had entailed no great breach of security.

He had then shaken the dust of London from his heels after closing up his town house.

Everything was done that could possibly have been done. He could not sit at leisure and hate Penelope Vesey as much as he wished. But his thoughts gradually became more troubled. He could not help remembering Penelope's pleading eyes and the fact that she had been fighting with Augusta when he had erupted onto the scene.

He got wearily to his feet and moved over to the desk at the window to go through his correspondence. Light snow was beginning to fall outside, dancing and swirling over the lawns, intensifying his strange feeling of isolation and loss.

Almost the first letter that came to hand was Penelope's express. In it she had poured out all her fear and anxiety. How she dared not go to the authorities because his brother's spying activities might be found out. She forgave him wholeheartedly for breaking the engagement. He would not, she said, wish to ally his great name to that of a girl who was related to a blackmailer, murderess, and spy. A cramped and tearstained postscript at the bottom seemed to leap out of the page. "I will always love you," Penelope had written, "and will always pray that you will come to forget me and find some suitable young lady of good family to be the mother of your children."

The Earl put down the letter slowly and stared unseeingly out at the now heavily falling snow. What a fool he had been! He had seen her again, only to lose her again.

He leaped into action, roaring for his horse and then taking the stairs five at a time to repack his bags.

Rourke gloomily watched his flying figure and selfishly hoped that he would not have to accompany his lordship this time. Enough was enough!

Penelope put down her needle with a sigh. The ball gown she had just completed spilled its silken lavender folds over her lap. Outside the sun shone merrily down on the snow-covered garden.

The girls were to attend their first ball that evening. Mrs. Jennings had insisted that Penelope go too. It was ridiculous, that good woman had said roundly, for Penelope to mope her life away when there were so many handsome fellows around.

The ball was to be held in the home of Mr. Delton, a wealthy brewer who lived in great style on the outskirts of Dover. In the mysterious way of society, beer was not considered to be "in trade," and so all the flower of the local county were expected to attend.

The waltz was now danced everywhere, and Penelope had made sure that her charges would be able to perform the dance with grace instead of turning it into a romp as they were wont to do.

Penelope had secretly hoped that the roads would be blocked, but the snow had stopped falling several days ago and the road to Dover was once again clear.

Nor would Mrs. Jennings hear of Penelope's plan to wear a turban and sit with the chaperones. How was she ever to get over that terrible Earl if she did not make an effort?

Mr. Jennings had met the Earl briefly in the magistrate's home and had been too relieved to hear that Penelope was exonerated to try to effect a reconciliation between the Earl and the girl.

Privately Mr. Jennings thought Penelope was well out of that engagement. The Earl was too haughty and austere to be the husband of such a young and pretty girl.

All too soon, the Jenningses' carriage was rolling along the hilly cobbled streets of Dover. Mr. Delton's town house was very grand indeed with a double row of steps rising up to an entrance on the first floor.

Flambeaux flickered, smoked, and blazed in the brackets outside, and the faint strains of a waltz reached Penelope's ears as she descended from the carriage.

The Deltons, husband and wife, were terrifyingly gracious and condescending, but Mrs. Jennings seemed to find nothing amiss except in the fact that the Deltons quite patently did not approve of Penelope being one of the party. Mrs. Delton ran one cold eye over Penelope from her blond hair to her fashionable lilac silk dress — too grand for a governess — and said in frigid tones that Miss . . . er . . . should sit with the chaperones. 'Twas more fitting.

Overawed and ill at ease, Mrs. Jennings had not the courage to argue, contenting herself with giving Penelope's hand a sympathetic squeeze.

Penelope did not know whether to be glad or sorry as she took her seat beside the row of middle-aged matrons.

About twenty couples were dancing energetically in the long room. Banks of artificial flowers, artificially scented, were massed against the walls which had been draped in rose silk for the occasion. Large fires crackled at either end of the room and tall branches of wax candles stared down at their reflections in the polished floor.

The fashions of the ladies were not so extreme as in London. There were no clinging muslins here, damped to reveal every inch of the wearer's form, no transparent dresses and scanty petticoats. Stiff formal taffetas, velvets, and merinos were the order of the day. The men were as colorfully dressed as the girls — Mr. Brummell's fashion for strict black and white in the ballroom having not yet penetrated as far as Dover — and many of them wore their hair powdered.

Penelope sat on, grimly counting her blessings. She had a good job and a comfortable home. But all the while a sly little feminine voice in her brain was telling her that it would be marvellous to have just *one* dance.

Apart from a perpetual aching feeling of loss, Penelope was already beginning to forget the horror of that day on the quay. Augusta already seemed part of some grotesque, feverish nightmare.

A footman hurried into the ballroom and accosted Mr. Delton, then both men hurriedly left the room. Mr. Delton reappeared after a few moments and summoned his wife and whispered in her ear.

Mrs. Delton turned and stared straight across the ballroom to where Penelope sat with a look of shock and surprise on her face. Then she too left the room.

Penelope looked sadly at her slippers. She had tried to tell Mrs. Jennings that silk lilac and an elaborate hairstyle were much too fine for a governess.

The quadrille came to a finish and Penelope had found some comfort in thinking that her charges had performed their parts competently.

The double doors at the end of the ballroom were flung open.

The Earl of Hestleton entered, flanked on either side by Mr. and Mrs. Delton.

He immediately made every man in the room look provincial and dowdy.

He was dressed in a close-fitting black silk evening coat, tailored by the great Weston. His black knee breeches and white stockings clung to his muscular legs and sapphires blazed from the snowy lace of his cravat and on the buckles of his shoes. He wore his auburn hair unpowdered, and his face looked

214

very severe and tense.

Penelope sat rigid in her chair, unable to look away. He had come to disgrace her! Why else would he look so severe, thought Penelope, mistaking the Earl's fatigue and apprehension for anger.

The couples had started to dance the waltz, and above their bobbing heads Penelope saw the Earl making his way round the edge of the ballroom towards her.

Suddenly Mrs. Jennings was at her side, her motherly face creased with worry. "It's that awful Earl again," she whispered. "I have talked with Mr. Jennings and he agrees I should take you straight home."

The Earl craned his head above the dancers and saw Penelope and Mrs. Jennings hurrying towards the door. He started forward, to push his way through the dancers, when, to his dismay, he was way-laid by the town magistrate, Mr. Henry Desmond. Mr. Desmond had proved to be very kind and helpful on the day of the deaths of Augusta and the Comte, and the Earl realised he could not cut him. He was forced to carry on a conversation with Mr. Desmond while the double doors of the ballroom opened and closed behind Penelope and Mrs. Jennings.

Well, at least he knew her address. As Mr.

Desmond talked on at length about the magisterial problems of his job, the Earl remembered his arrival in Dover only that evening. He had obtained Mr. Jennings's direction from the landlord of the Green Man and had then ridden hard to Wold, only to find the house empty except for the servants who told him that the Jenningses and their governess had gone to the Deltons' ball in Dover.

Another gruelling ride back to Dover and more lost time while he changed into his evening clothes, although he would have preferred to defy the conventions in the manner of young Lochinvar and ride into the ballroom on his horse.

He set his mind to extracting himself from the magistrate's company. Then there was a tedious period of time to be endured trying to escape from his hosts. Finally he managed to corner Mr. Jennings and ask that very surprised gentleman permission to pay his addresses to Penelope.

"I'm not really sure," said Mr. Jennings in his maddeningly slow and precise way. "Let us examine the case . . ."

And the Earl answered his questions patiently while inside his angry soul screamed and consigned the whole of the legal profession to hell.

"I think it would be best," said Mr. Jennings finally, "if you called on Miss Vesey in the morning. I will tell her that your intentions are honorable and that I have given you my permission — for what it is worth — to pay your addresses." He looked up at the Earl's hard face and gave a little sigh. "However, my lord, if you will take the advice of an older man, I would suggest you look less *angry* when you go a-courting."

"I am not angry," said the Earl between his teeth. "Only frustrated."

"Dear me!" exclaimed Mr. Jennings, quite shocked. "In your suit, I trust, and not in your passions."

"In both," said the Earl grimly.

"Dear me," said Mr. Jennings again. "How free-spoken is the youth of today! Not that you are by any means a youth, my lord. In fact I would say you were considerably older than Miss Vesey. In fact . . ."

"I am not in my dotage," snapped the Earl.

"Well, well, I did not say that. What a bad-tempered man you are, to be sure. Don't look so toplofty, my lord. I realise my remarks might be construed as impertinent, but I assure you, I and my wife have come to love Miss Vesey very much and look on her as a daughter."

His lordship gave a faint sigh and then set himself to please. Nothing could come of antagonising Penelope's employer. The Deltons observed the conversation from afar, wondering what on earth the Earl could find to amuse himself in such undistinguished company! And why had he said that he wished to speak to the Jenningses' governess?

The Earl duly presented himself at the Jenningses house at nine o'clock the following morning to be met by Mrs. Jennings, still wearing her nightcap and quite shocked that any gentleman should call at such an early hour. He must wait until Penelope was dressed and prepared to see him.

Mrs. Jennings knew that Penelope had finally fallen asleep at dawn after a restless night of worry. Mr. Jennings had decided not to tell Penelope of the Earl's honorable intentions. She must make up her own mind when she saw him without anyone else influencing her, he had said. And Mrs. Jennings was determined that Penelope should have her beauty sleep before she faced the ordeal ahead of her for, in her heart, Mrs. Jennings was sure Penelope would refuse the haughty Earl.

The Earl waited patiently for two hours in

the sitting room, stretched out in an arm-chair in front of the fire. He finally closed his eyes and fell asleep.

And that was how Penelope found him when she timidly opened the door.

She crossed quietly to the armchair and stood looking down at him. He looked much younger asleep and somehow vulner-able. She stretched out her hand slowly and gently stroked the copper curls. His eyes flew open and he imprisoned her hand in a strong grasp.

A strong current of attraction ran from one hand to the other until both were trembling. All the hates and doubts seemed to disappear like magic. He forgot about all the long speeches of love and desire he had so carefully rehearsed and got to his feet and pulled her urgently into his arms, kissing her until she was breathless.

"We've been mad," he murmured huskily. "Absolutely mad. I want you more than any-thing in the world, Penelope. Will you marry me?" He gave her a little shake. "You must marry me."

"But I am related to a murderess," whis-pered Penelope. "You must think of your name."

"A pox on my name," said the Earl. "Con-cern for the Hestleton name started all this mess. I am not asking you to marry me, Penelope. I am telling you that you are going to marry me. No other man is ever going to touch you. I'm jealous of everybody who even looks at you."

He drew her down on to a hard horsehair sofa covered in shiny leather. "What do you say?" he whispered intensely.

"Oh, yes, Roger," said Penelope thankfully, sinking into his arms. She gave a sudden giggle. "How do you know I am not a murderess too? I might put rat poison in your port." Her hand flew to her mouth and her face blanched. "How can I joke about such things! Did I tell you of Aunt Augusta's poor footman! She — she *poisoned* him. How shall I ever forget?"

"Like this," he whispered into her hair. He turned her mouth up to his and covered her lips in a long, long kiss which sent both their senses reeling.

Penelope recovered enough to feel herself slipping from the shiny sofa onto the uncarpeted floor. She clutched wildly at the Earl's shoulders and both of them landed on the floor with an undignified bump.

"Now," said the Earl, smiling wickedly into her eyes, "I have you just where I want you."

The frenzy of their lovemaking rose to

fever pitch. "Why do women have these damned little buttons on their dresses?" murmured the Earl at one point, his voice sounding in his ears strangely unlike his own.

Penelope smiled tantalisingly up into his eyes. "To stop making things too easy for the gentlemen, I suppose," she giggled.

"I shall persevere," said the Earl, reaching his long fingers to the little buttons at the throat of her Kerseymere gown. "There is one, there is another . . . and another . . . and . . ."

"MY LORD!"

The Jenningses' husband and wife stood in the doorway, rigid with shock.

The guilty couple rose hurriedly to their feet.

The Earl took Penelope's hand in his own.

"We are to be married in a month's time," he said to the horrified Jenningses. "I am taking Miss Vesey to Wyndham Court today. We shall be married from there."

"Such goings-on!" said Mrs. Jennings severely. "Miss Vesey is not going anywhere without being chaperoned and so I tell you. Mr. Jennings and I will be there to see Miss Vesey married as she should be, especially after your abandoned behavior, my lord."

"My Aunt Matilda is in residence and will

be chaperone enough," said the Earl coldly.

"So you say," replied Mrs. Jennings, equally coldly. "Mr. Jennings, tell the servants to make ready. You are having us as houseguests, my lord, whether you like it or not!"

Chapter Fourteen

The Earl began to feel as if he had never been so closely guarded in his life. Everywhere he turned, there seemed to be a watchful eye.

Aunt Matilda had confided to the Jenningses that she considered her nephew flighty. First the engagement was on, then it was off, then it was on again. For Penelope's sake, the proprieties must be observed.

Everywhere the Earl and Penelope went at Wyndham Court, a Jennings went too. Aunt Matilda had developed the unnerving habit of popping into Penelope's bedroom at all hours of the night and running her fingers over the pillows to make sure that the bed only contained one body.

Jane and Alice considered it great sport, a new exciting sort of game, and took turns to dog Penelope's footsteps whenever she strayed from the house.

But the guardians arose one morning to find the couple had fled and the Earl would not have been at all flattered to hear the discussion on his manners and morals which went on throughout the day.

"I think it is *quite* shocking," said Aunt Matilda, oblivious to warning looks from Mrs. Jennings who was afraid her daughters were becoming overtitillated by all this racy conversation. "I mean," went on Aunt Matilda, "they are shortly to be married after all. But Roger was always *very dangerous* with regard to the female . . . er . . . sex. Now, I remember that little opera dancer he had in keeping . . ." She broke off and bit her lip.

"Oh, *do* tell," cried Jane and Alice, their eyes shining.

"Yes, do tell," remarked a mocking voice from the doorway.

All stared in amazement. The Earl was standing there with a radiant Penelope on his arm.

He drew a piece of paper out of his pocket and threw it on the table.

"Allow me to present you all with our marriage lines. We were married today by special license.

"And now, if you will excuse me, my wife and I are very tired and would like to go to . . ."

"Bed," said Aunt Matilda in a shocked whisper while Penelope blushed red and stared at the floor in pretty confusion.

"Exactly," smiled the Earl. "And as we are very, very, *very* tired, we do not wish to be disturbed for days and days and days. Come, my dear!" He led the still blushing Penelope from the room, and there was a long silence after the doors had closed behind the happy couple.

Mr. Jennings gave a self-conscious laugh. "They are *married* after all," he said.

"Why, so they are," said Mrs. Jennings with a sudden smile, "and here we all are sitting round like a church meeting."

"It *does* change things," said Aunt Matilda seriously. "It makes it all less . . . well, you know . . . *embarrassing*.

"After all, one's poor imagination does not follow them into the bedroom when they are married, don't you think?"

Jane and Alice giggled wildly.

"Girls! Go to your rooms," said Mrs. Jennings severely. Penelope was not setting a very good example for her impressionable daughters. Not one little bit!

The employees of Thorndike Press hope you have enjoyed this Large Print book. All our Large Print titles are designed for easy reading, and all our books are made to last. Other Thorndike Press Large Print books are available at your library, through selected bookstores, or directly from us.

For information about titles, please call:

(800) 223-1244
(800) 223-6121

To share your comments, please write:

Publisher
Thorndike Press
295 Kennedy Memorial Drive
Waterville, ME   04901